T0357379

Meet Me at Blue Hour

ALSO BY SARAH SUK

Made in Korea
The Space between Here & Now

Meet Me at Blue Hour

Sarah Suk

Quill Tree Books

An Imprint of HarperCollinsPublishers

Quill Tree Books is an imprint of HarperCollins Publishers.

Meet Me at Blue Hour
Copyright © 2025 by Sarah Suk
All rights reserved. Manufactured in Harrisonburg,
VA, United States of America.
No part of this book may be used or reproduced in any manner
whatsoever without written permission except in the case of
brief quotations embodied in critical articles and reviews. For
information address HarperCollins Children's Books, a division of
HarperCollins Publishers, 195 Broadway, New York, NY 10007.
www.epicreads.com

Library of Congress Control Number: 2024950197
ISBN 978-0-06-325518-0

Typography by David Curtis
24 25 26 27 28 LBC 5 4 3 2 1
First Edition

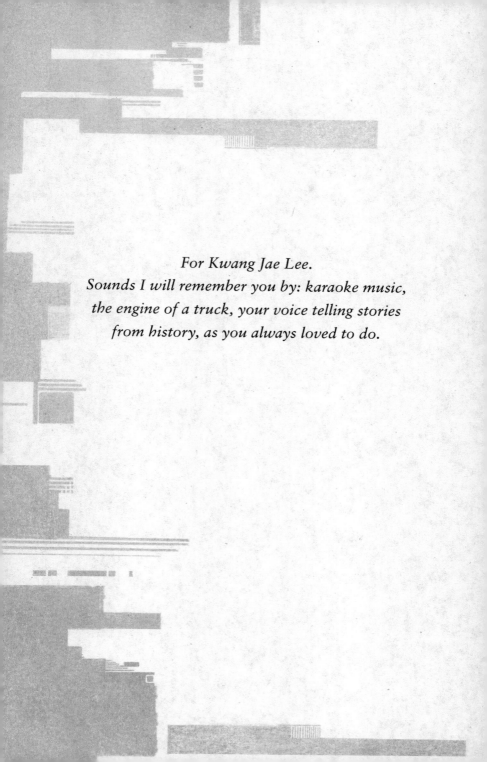

For Kwang Jae Lee.
Sounds I will remember you by: karaoke music,
the engine of a truck, your voice telling stories
from history, as you always loved to do.

Meet Me at Blue Hour

1

YENA

These are the sounds they used for forgetting: train whistles, suitcase wheels on cobblestone, raindrops pattering against an open umbrella. To me, it all seems awfully romantic, something I could replay a thousand times over—and I have. Of all the mixtapes I've listened to, this one is by far my favorite. But to Patient 1562 it was more than just sounds on a cassette tape. It was a memory they wanted to erase.

"I wonder what it was." I pull my earphones out, draping the cord around my neck, and lean back against the wall from where I'm sitting on the floor, surrounded by cardboard boxes full of tapes. Danielle Flores, my supervisor, pokes her head out from behind a stack of boxes, a laptop perched precariously on top of them.

"What are you talking about?" she says, a strand of dark curly hair falling over her forehead. She blows it out of her eyes.

"Patient 1562." I open the Walkman clipped to the waistband of my denim shorts, pull out the tape, tuck it back into its plastic case with a dreamy sigh. "I wonder what the memory they erased was. It sounds so beautiful, but it was probably a sad one if they wanted to forget."

Danielle presses her fingers against her temples and lets out a slow, deep breath. "Yena, are you telling me that you've been listening to tapes this whole time instead of, oh, I don't know, doing your actual job?"

"Um . . . I mean, not the *whole* time."

It's only been a week since I started my job at Sori of Us Clinic, or just Sori Clinic for short, as their new archive assistant—a title that is way fancier than the actual work itself—and I can't say my supervisor has been too keen to have me on board. It's not that I don't have the makings to be Employee of the Month or anything, but how excited can I be to organize thousands of mixtapes when I can listen to them instead?

Before Danielle can unleash the fury of her ever-growing migraine on me, there's a light knock on the door and Dr. Mira Bae steps in, holding a box of Dunkin' Donuts. I quickly stumble to my feet, unclipping the Walkman and holding it behind my back, earphones bunched in one hand. Dr. Bae smiles at both of us, and then she sees the look on Danielle's face.

"Just wanted to see how things are going in here," she says. Her voice is cheerful, but she's shooting daggers at me with her eyes.

"Hi, Dr. Bae. Things are going just fine," Danielle says. Bless her soul. A stickler for the rules she may be, but a snitch she is not. "Are those donuts?"

She hurries over to take the box, receiving it with both hands. As the founder of the clinic and one of the top researchers in the field of memory erasure, Dr. Mira Bae has the deeply earned respect of everyone in the building and beyond. She is a genius, a boss, a trailblazer with the most perfectly manicured nails you've ever seen.

"Danielle, I hope my daughter isn't giving you too hard a time," she says.

Oh. And she's also my mom.

Danielle laughs, waving a hand in the air. "No, no, not at all. She's doing great."

"So great," I add. "The Memotery has never looked better." Dr. Bae raises her eyebrows and I quickly correct myself. "The Archive, I mean. The Archive has never looked better."

I think of this room in many names. Formally, it's the Mixtape Archive, but to me, it's the Library of Sounds, the Place for the Forgotten, or my personal favorite, the Memotery, a combination of the words *memory* and *cemetery*, the final place where one's erased history goes to rest.

In the early days, the Memotery used to be one overflowing storage closet with rickety built-in shelves at the clinic and an impressive collection of cardboard boxes stuffed to the brim with cassette tapes stored in my mom's Busan apartment, leaning against the refrigerator, occupying the guest bedroom, working overtime as both a TV stand and a coffee table in the living room. Even now, I'll sometimes find the occasional tape strewn around the house, lost memories wedged between the couch cushions or tucked behind the toaster.

But eventually, as Sori Clinic's reputation grew, so did their office space. This year, they finally got an upgrade with a new, shiny room dedicated to storing the tapes with new, shiny shelving and a new, shiny job title for the person in charge of organizing it all: the archivist. And the archive assistant.

The former was a part-time role they actively hired, and the latter was created just for me because Dr. Bae would not have her only daughter graduate from high school with no college plans or future aspirations, no ma'am. If I didn't have any plans, my mom would make some for me and put me to work until I did, which was how I found myself packing my bags after graduation and flying across the ocean from Vancouver, Canada, to Busan, South Korea, to join her at her clinic for the summer.

"I hope I'm not overstepping, but is this really a two-person job?" Danielle said when I first began. "I can take care of organizing the Archive on my own."

"I'm confident you can, Danielle, but think of how much quicker it'll be with an assistant," Dr. Bae said. "Besides, I'm hoping you'll be a good influence on my daughter here. Yena, did you know Danielle is a writer? And she's here from America, studying at Pusan National University for a year! I did an exchange just like that when I was in undergrad. Doesn't that sound like fun? Maybe you'd want to do an exchange program one day?"

Subtlety. It's not what Dr. Bae is famous for.

I watch the two of them now, chatting enthusiastically. I can tell by the sideways glance in my direction and the way she raises her voice when she asks Danielle how school is going that she wants me to listen, to be curious, to want what Danielle has: a field to study, a passion to pursue. Something. Anything.

Instead, I look up to the ceiling and picture trains on a rainy day, tuning out their voices. For a second, I'm not in this room full of empty shelves and cardboard boxes. I'm in someone else's story, imagining things they'll never remember again.

"Well, keep up the good work, Danielle," Dr. Bae says as their conversation dwindles down. "Will you be joining the team dinner tonight?"

Danielle shakes her head. "Unfortunately, no. I have a big paper I have to get going on."

Dr. Bae nods in understanding. "I won't be able to make it myself. Still a lot to prepare for our clinic's upcoming study. Yena, how about you?"

I blink, trying to catch up on what I missed. "Sorry, what?"

"The monthly staff dinner that Joanne organized. Are you going?"

"Oh. No."

I don't bother giving a reason. What is there to say? It's not that I have other plans or work to catch up on. Team dinners just aren't really my thing and it's not like I know the other staff at the clinic that well anyway.

"All right," Dr. Bae says after a beat of awkward silence. "I'll see you at home tonight, Yena. Don't wait up for me. I'll be staying late at the office."

I can count on one hand the number of times we've had a meal together since I arrived in Busan, and I wouldn't even need all five fingers. By now, I've come to understand that staying late and going early to work is basically her daily routine.

"Yes, Dr. Bae," I say, giving her a salute with my free hand, the other still holding the Walkman behind my back.

She leaves and Danielle opens the box of donuts, holding it out to me. "Sounds like your mom is still on your case about university," she says.

"Even you can tell?" I take out a donut that's in the shape of a bear's head and look somberly at its face. "My god, what have her conversation skills come to."

"Out of curiosity, what *do* you want to do?" Danielle asks. "Because you clearly don't want to be working here."

"I'm still young. Did you know what you wanted to do with your life when you were seventeen?"

"Yes. I wanted to write."

"Well, you're a bad example of the point I'm trying to

make." I shrug. "I don't know yet. And maybe I'll never know. Besides, does it even matter? Nothing lasts forever. Just because I have a dream today doesn't mean it will mean anything tomorrow, so what's the point of making all these plans?"

Danielle cocks her head to the side. "Interesting."

"What?"

"Nothing. It just seems quite contrary to your mom's philosophy of life," she says. "She's probably the most committed and passionate person I've ever met. Kind of ironic that her daughter is the opposite."

She says it in a matter-of-fact way, as if simply making an observation, but something about her choice of words stings.

I push the feeling away, stuffing the bear donut into my mouth. I dust my hands off, swallow, give Danielle a toothy grin. "Shall we get back to organizing these tapes?"

"Get back to?" Danielle says with a pointed look.

"I can be a good worker when I want to be."

And I am for the rest of my shift. I help Danielle organize all the mixtapes by patient number and then by year of erasure, pruning out all the tapes that are older than a decade by cross-checking them with the database of patient information on Danielle's laptop. But even as I work, going through the movements of sorting through box after box, I can't stop thinking about what she said.

The opposite of committed and passionate. It bothers

7

me more than I want it to. Is that really me?

Funny. It didn't used to be.

It starts with a sound.

That's Sori Clinic's official motto, the header at the top of their website, the phrase embossed on their business cards. *Sori* is the Korean word for "sound," and it alludes to the process of erasure itself. In order to forget something, a patient has to bring in a collection of sounds related to the memory they want to erase. Voice memos, songs, background recordings, anything. The more specific they are to the exact memory the better, but general sounds that trigger enough associations can do the job just as well. The process truly begins not when the patient is in the operating chair but when they start collecting sounds.

It also alludes to the new beginnings that erasure offers, which is what Sori Clinic is all about. Fresh starts and healing.

I can see the temptation in that.

The July afternoon heat is sticky and humid against my skin as I walk along the shore of Haeundae Beach, phone in one hand, the straps of my sandals dangling from the other. I stare at the phone screen as it rings, and a moment later, Dad's familiar bearded face appears on the screen.

"Hi, Yena Bean! How are you?" he says. In the background, I can see the overflowing bookshelf in the living room of our Vancouver apartment, filled with potted plants and his collection of gardening books. Even through Face-Time, I can tell that all the plants look as shiny as ever, thriving under the care of his green thumb, though it looks like the sagging shelves could use some of that same TLC. I can also tell that there's a woman's cardigan I've never seen before hanging off the back of the couch in my field of vision. I don't mention it.

"Or maybe a better question is, where are you?" he says. "Looks nice over there."

"Hi, Dad. I'm at Haeundae." I duck my head out of the frame so he can see the ocean behind me, panning the phone across the crowded beach to show all the people strolling along the sand, taking selfies, and sitting under beach umbrellas. It's absolutely packed here today, but I don't mind. "I like to come here after work sometimes."

"Joketda," he says wistfully. "Do you know what that means?"

"Please, that's too easy. It means you're super jealous of me, right?" I say with a teasing grin.

"Ohhh, sounds like your Korean's getting pretty good there," Dad says, looking impressed.

Having grown up with both parents speaking English to me, my Korean language abilities lie somewhere on the spectrum between basic and barely there, even with my brief stint going to Korean school on Saturdays as a kid. It's not a problem at Sori Clinic, which operates on an entirely bilingual system (and an entirely English one between me and Danielle, though her Korean is admittedly much more impressive than mine), but outside of that, it's probably a good idea for me to try to pick it up a bit more.

"So, what's going on?" Dad asks. He tries to appear casual, but I can tell by the way he leans forward a little with his eyebrows knit together that he knows something is off. He's pretty good at that. Though I guess the fact that I'm calling at all might have clued him in. We haven't talked much since I came to Korea, save for the big updates like *I'm alive* and *I made it in one piece.* "Everything okay?"

"Dad, do I have commitment issues?" I ask.

He blinks at the screen and for a second, I think he's frozen.

"Dad?"

"Sorry, I'm here. I was just wondering what you mean by that?"

"I mean, it's nothing really. Just something my supervisor said to me," I say. "Well, to be exact, she said I'm the opposite of committed, which obviously means commitment issues. And she also said I'm not passionate! Can you believe her? That's so rude, right?"

Dad is silent. I frown and shake the phone, trying to reset him. "Hello?"

"I'm still here," he says. After a pause, he adds, "I'm sure she didn't mean anything negative by it, Yena. Perhaps she was just commenting on your free-spirited and laid-back nature."

I narrow my eyes at him. "You agree."

He sighs. "Well, Bean, you don't exactly stick to anything or anyone for very long. At least not since Lucas moved away. You haven't been the same since."

And there it is. Even after all these years, hearing his name makes my stomach feel like it's falling through my feet. I look away from the phone.

"I have no idea what you're talking about," I say.

It starts with a sound.

For me and Lucas Pak, it started with the *pop pop pop* of the movie theater popcorn machine, the birthplace of our friendship. From the ages of eleven to fourteen, we were inseparable. He was my best friend and I was his, a truth sealed by pinkie promises, thumbs stamped together, a string of bike rides, bruised knees, film nights, secrets only he and I knew. It was the closest I'd ever been to being a mind reader, to having my mind read. That's how well we knew each other.

And then one day, he disappeared without a word, and I realized I didn't know him very well at all. The Lucas I knew would have answered my confused texts, would have picked up my calls, would have told me before leaving the province and vanishing from my life as if he were nothing but a magic trick. Now you see him, now you don't.

I had to hear through the grapevine that he and his family had taken off to Alberta. Honestly, if I hadn't heard that, I would have thought he was dead. How does someone go from being your best friend to completely ghosting you? I couldn't wrap my mind around it and, nearly four years later, the thought still makes me gloomy as hell. I feel pathetic every time it crosses my mind. I should be over this by now.

"I don't even really remember him," I lie. "And I can stick to things. I just haven't found the right thing or person that I click with yet. But I can definitely do it."

"Well, I hope your time in Korea will help with that," Dad says sincerely. He clears his throat. "So, how's your mom doing these days?"

Talking to Dad about Mom and vice versa is probably my least favorite pastime, but I don't want to think about Lucas anymore, so I let him change the subject. "She's fine. Not the happiest with my life decisions, but otherwise thriving."

"I bet she blames me for those life decisions, doesn't she?" Dad says, scoffing.

"Please, Dad," I say, rolling my eyes. What I don't say is that she may have mentioned that very sentiment once or twice since I came to Korea. Maybe more. Who's counting? Not me. "What did I tell you about putting me in the middle of your divorce and any resulting complicated feelings regarding it?"

"You said don't do it."

"Exactly."

We chat a little longer on more neutral topics like how his gardening business is doing and whether Greg, the cat next door who likes to come over to our apartment for weeks at a time, will stop leaving dead mice on the balcony. After we say goodbye and hang up, I stand still, staring out at the water.

It's possible that both Danielle and Dad aren't completely wrong about me. For all the parties and school clubs I hopped around in high school, I never really made a friend who went deeper than a good time and an Instagram follow or had an interest that lasted longer than a week. It's never bugged me before. I've never even thought about it—it just was what it was. But then, I've never heard it out loud like this before either.

"Which character would you be?" I remember asking Lucas on one of our film nights. We were huddled on the couch with a giant bowl of pretzels, doing a marathon of all three Lord of the Rings movies. Even more than watching the films themselves, I loved imagining myself in them, walking through the story as my own main character.

"I don't know, but I know who you would be." He pointed a pretzel at me and grinned. "Aragorn."

My heart fluttered. Aragorn was my favorite character. "Because we both have amazing hair?"

"That. And because you're the most loyal and dedicated person I know, and you'd take a sword for anyone."

When Lucas left, did he take that Aragorn piece of me with him? I hate thinking that, the idea that he could have such an impact on me when I had so little on him. People who don't care about you anymore shouldn't still get to hold on to pieces of you.

I turn away from the water, the sun hot against the back of my neck as I trudge through the sand with new determination in my step. Maybe Dad thinks I haven't been the same since Lucas, but I'll show him how untrue that is, how over it I am. He and Danielle can both just wait and see.

2

LUCAS

In any new situation, it's important to have a plan. That way, you can leave as little room for error as possible.

I look down at the Notes app on my phone where I wrote out my plan for arriving in Korea. It reads:

> Fly into Incheon International Airport. Review Umma's new menu for the restaurant while on the plane. Make notes to email her when I have Wi-Fi. One-hour layover at the airport. Get a snack, stretch, brush teeth. Update Umma and Appa on how the travel is going. Send email.
> Flight to Busan. Arrive at Gimhae International Airport at 6:00 p.m. Update Umma and Appa again. Samchon should be waiting at Arrivals to pick me up.

Of course, even with a plan as simple as this one, things can go wrong. Like your uncle forgetting to pick you up when he said he would.

"Ah, Lucas! Are you here already?" Samchon says, answering my call in Korean with a jovial, booming voice.

"Yes, I am. Are you?" I reply also in Korean, looking around. My palm is sweaty against the handle of my carry-on suitcase as I wheel it over to a bench away from the crowd. I haven't seen my uncle in a long time and I'm not sure he would recognize me. The last time I visited Korea, I was probably half the height I am now. "I'm wearing a gray T-shirt." In the time it takes me to say that sentence, five other guys in gray T-shirts walk by me. Very helpful.

"Yes, sorry. Almost there. I wanted to be waiting right at the gate holding a sign with your name on it, but your grandpa wanted a coffee," Samchon chuckles.

"Wait. Harabeoji's here?" I say. "I told him to wait for me at home!"

"And you think I'd listen to you?" a gravelly voice behind me says.

I whirl around to see the all-too-familiar face of my grandfather grinning at me, holding two cups of coffee in his hands. He gives me one, patting me on the back.

"Full of cream and sugar just the way you like it, you monster," he says.

A wave of emotion wells up in my chest. Is it the fact that he remembers my coffee order? Or is it hearing his voice, so familiar, speaking in a mix of Korean and English like we always do when we talk to each other? I fold him into a hug. "I thought I told you not to come out," I say, but

I can't help the smile that tugs at the corners of my lips.

"Yeah, yeah, I'm happy to see you too." He takes a step back and examines me. "So this is what a high school graduate looks like. Thought it'd be more impressive, to be honest."

"What are you talking about? I can't believe this good-looking young man is my nephew!" Samchon says, appearing behind Harabeoji holding a paper sign that says LUCAS PAK on it.

"Oh, Samchon. You literally made a sign," I say, cheeks warming in embarrassment.

"Of course I did. It's your first time visiting me in Busan!" he says. "Honestly, I'm surprised your parents let you travel on your own. I know how cautious they can be when it comes to you. Least I can do is give you a proper welcome."

Cautious is probably an understatement when it comes to describing my parents. Speaking of, I quickly send them a text letting them know I've met up with Samchon before sticking my phone into my pocket.

Samchon seizes my suitcase and starts wheeling it across the airport. "Come on, the car's this way! Your grandpa was really looking forward to seeing you, you know. He's having a good day today too. Must be because he knew you were coming."

Harabeoji takes a sip of his coffee and leisurely follows along. I hurry after them both.

It's only been six months since I last saw him, but that's

the longest we've ever been apart. Before moving back to Korea to live with Samchon earlier this year, Harabeoji lived with me and my parents in Canada. He was there by my side ever since I was a kid. It's been strange not having him in the house anymore. I watch his back moving ahead of me now, try to notice all the ways he's changed since he left.

Maybe he's gotten shorter.

Maybe his hair has gotten whiter.

Maybe his Alzheimer's has gotten worse.

I shake the thought out of my head. No, I won't worry about that. I've done enough worrying ever since he was officially diagnosed late last year. Besides, I didn't come all the way to Korea to stress about how he might be getting worse.

I'm here to make sure he doesn't.

We squeeze into Samchon's car, Harabeoji in the front passenger seat and me in the back with the big LUCAS PAK sign. Harabeoji fiddles with the audio and starts playing the Beatles.

"Did you know, Lucas, your uncle was so surprised that I know how to use Bluetooth," he says, sounding smug. "Weren't you, Taehoon?"

"I was. Honestly, he's better with technology than me," Samchon says. "He said you taught him everything he knows, Lucas."

"It's nothing," I say.

"It's amazing is what it is," Harabeoji says. "I was able to watch your graduation from all the way across the world because it was livestreamed. If that's not the future, what is?"

Samchon snorts. "You should have seen him with his nose up to the computer screen. Had his phone out and everything to record the moment you walked across the stage."

"I know. He sent it to me on KakaoTalk," I say, laughing. "It's a very zoomed-in video."

If there was one thing that made Harabeoji hesitate about moving back to Korea, it was missing my graduation. He's always been big on celebrating milestones and he really wanted to be at the ceremony. You only graduate from high school once, he said. But the way timing and logistics worked out, it made more sense for him to leave before then.

"That zoomed-in video is proof of your education," Harabeoji says sternly. "There's nothing more important than that. Turn up the music, Taehoon."

Samchon does, and Harabeoji begins to sing along. I lean my head back on the headrest, the exhaustion from the travel day catching up to me. I don't sleep well on planes, but there's something about cars that always gets me dozing, like a child being rocked back and forth.

I close my eyes and let Harabeoji's singing carry me off to sleep.

It's 5:00 a.m. when I jolt awake with a gasp, sweating from the nightmare I'd been having. I'm lying on the couch in Samchon's living room, tangled up in a blanket. It takes me a second to remember how I got here. I vaguely recall walking up to his apartment after grabbing dinner at a nearby soondubu restaurant, insisting that I'd sleep on the couch after Samchon repeatedly offered me his room. I'm pretty sure I knocked out immediately as soon as my head hit the pillow.

I sit up, unraveling the blanket from my legs. The nightmare is a recurring one. In it, I'm swimming in pitch-dark waters and then something wraps around my knees, my ankles, and pulls me down, down, down into the depths. Sometimes I manage to escape it, sometimes I don't, but the feeling of fear and panic is always the same.

I try to shake the feeling off now and reach for my phone. The brightness from the screen makes me squint.

There are several messages and voice notes from my parents, including Umma's reply to my email about the menu. I skip it for now, opening my web browser instead and searching up *Busan Sori of Us Clinic*.

I go to their website, scrolling straight past their FAQ and Testimonial pages to the section titled Memory Recovery Clinical Study, a page I've visited more times than I can count since I first found it. I don't know if it's habit or a need for reassurance, but I read through it again now, nearly mouthing the words along by heart.

Sori of Us Clinic (commonly referred to as Sori Clinic) specializes in erasing memories through sound, but what if we could also restore lost memories through the same method? That's the question we are exploring in this clinical study.

We are looking for people diagnosed with memory loss including but not limited to dementia, Alzheimer's, and short-term memory loss to participate in this study. To be eligible, participants must have a companion available to assist them in the gathering of old memories that participants may not be able to recall themselves.

The study will be held in Busan, South Korea, at our clinic's office. Participants must be available to attend in person for a period of at least two months.

Update: Due to an overwhelming amount of interest, all slots in the study are currently full. If you'd like to hear about any openings in future studies, please join our online waitlist. Thank you very much for all your support. Here's to the future of memories.

After Harabeoji was diagnosed with Alzheimer's, he wanted to move back to Korea to spend as much time as he had left in the country where he grew up. I didn't want him to go, couldn't imagine a life where I didn't see him every day, waking up under the same roof, but how could I say no? As devastated as I was, I wanted Harabeoji to be happy, and this was what would make him happy.

So arrangements were made for him to live with Sam-chon, who had just relocated from Seoul to Busan for a promotion. He had a bigger apartment, and the money to hire a caretaker to look after Harabeoji when he was at work. With my own parents busy running their restaurant, it made the most sense for everybody. But still, it felt like the end of something, the end of everything.

I spent hours, days, weeks researching everything I could about Alzheimer's, reading about the different stages, looking for cures that didn't exist. And then I discovered Sori Clinic and their recovery study, and for the first time since Harabeoji's diagnosis, I felt a glimmer of hope.

The clinic was in Busan, where Harabeoji was. If this wasn't fate, what was?

The study was already full when I found it, but that didn't deter me. First, I signed up for the waitlist. Then I convinced my parents to let me visit Harabeoji for the summer as a graduation trip. The rest of my plan is this:

While I'm in Korea, I'll visit Sori Clinic every day to try to get him off the waitlist and into the study. There are bound to be people who drop out and spots that open up, and when there are, I'll be the first one there to claim that spot.

Over the summer, I'll assist him in the study to recover his memories. Harabeoji doesn't know what I'm up to yet, but if all goes according to plan, he will soon. And everything will be okay.

I get up from the couch and go into the kitchen, turning on the stove light. The clinic doesn't open until 9:00 a.m.

so until then, I calm my racing mind by washing some rice, rooting through Samchon's fridge, and pulling out a block of tofu, green onions, soy sauce, busying my hands with making breakfast for three.

I'll cook. I'll eat. And then I'll go to Sori Clinic to save my grandpa's memories.

SOUND

THE POPCORN MACHINE
11 YEARS OLD

Sure, I remember them. Those two kids dressed up in cosplay for the special Studio Ghibli screening at the theater, right?

I remember everyone. I've been here a long time.

She was dressed up as some character, all black robes and white face paint with purple lines down her cheeks, staring at me from the counter. Kind of creepy. But also, a little endearing, the way she was leaning forward, entranced, head bobbing slightly in time with the *pop pop pop* of my dance. It's nice to have fans.

She looked around for her father, who was standing by the butter machine, chatting with a woman and laughing. I could see the dilemma on her face. She wanted to ask him for a bag of popcorn, but she didn't want to interrupt him.

"Look, Lucas," an older gentleman in line said to the boy at his side. "That girl is dressed up for the movie too. And you were worried you'd be the only one!"

The boy is wearing some kind of gray animal costume with whiskers drawn on his face and a black circle on his nose, which I can only assume was meant to be a nose on a nose. He looked shyly at the girl, who must have felt him staring because she turned to look at him too. She gasped, running up to him.

"I love your Totoro costume!" she exclaimed.

"I like your No Face costume too," he said, partially hiding behind the older gentleman's leg. He smiled.

She peered more closely at him. "You look kind of familiar. Do you go to Korean school on Saturdays? The one next to the noodle place?"

"Um, yeah, I do. Do you?"

"Yes! I think I've seen you during recess. I recognize your face. You probably wouldn't recognize mine right now though."

I guess you could say I was the soundtrack to their first conversation. Their voices blended with my own and the sound of sodas pouring, candy wrappers crinkling, footsteps shuffling forward in line. The older gentleman bought a bag of popcorn for the boy. The girl looked wistfully back at her father, still wrapped up in his own conversation.

"Wow, the popcorn is way bigger than I thought," the boy said. He cleared his throat, glancing at the girl. "Do you want to sit next to us in the theater and share? I mean, you don't have to. Just if you want to. And if Harabeoji's okay with it."

"I think that's a great idea," the older gentleman said.

"I *love* sharing!" the girl said enthusiastically. Her father had finally ended his chat and was looking for her. She waved at him from across the theater, hollering, "Dad! We're going to sit next to my new friend!"

She bounded forward with the boy at her side, both still humming with excited conversation, their steps in time to my pop pop popping in a dance of their own.

3

YENA

According to Google, running is a great hobby for someone who doesn't have any. All you need is a good pair of running shoes, which I don't have, but lucky for me, Dr. Bae and I are the same size.

I can hear her doing her makeup in the bathroom, door slightly ajar, when I roll out of bed to find her. It's way earlier than I normally wake up and my eyes are bleary from staying up too late researching how to be a more dedicated person. But if I want to catch Mom before she goes to work, this is the time to do it. I yawn, about to knock on the door before poking my head in when I hear her speak.

My hand hovers in the air. Is she on the phone with someone? I peer through the crack in the door and see her lean closer to the mirror, eyeliner in hand. I don't see a phone anywhere and she's not wearing earphones. Is she talking to herself?

"I know you're worried and there are still a lot of unknowns, but remember, that's the point of a study.

Research wouldn't be so important if we already knew everything, right?" she says to her reflection. She finishes her makeup and takes a step back, studying her face. Her eyes grow steely, resolute. "You've made breakthroughs in the field before, and you'll do it again. You have to. You can do this, Mira."

I turn, shuffling a few steps away from the bathroom just as she swings the door open. She startles, hand flying to her chest.

"Jesus, Yena. What are you doing up so early?"

"Um . . . shoes!" I say, trying not to let on that I was eavesdropping. "Do you have any I can borrow?"

Her brow furrows in confusion. "You'll have to be a little more clear. What kind of shoes?"

"Running shoes. I'm going to be a runner starting today." I put my hands on my hips, smile with confidence. She just stares at me, confusion growing.

"O . . . kay . . . I think I have an extra pair in the closet. I'm running late though so you'll have to look for them yourself."

I glance at the clock on the wall, a vintage pink circular piece that looks more like it belongs in a '50s diner than in my mom's bland apartment. It's the only personal touch she has in the whole place, though I'm not sure what the story behind it is, and it's telling me that it's not even 6:30 a.m. yet.

"Well, I was thinking of jogging to work today," I say, following her as she hurries to the front door, grabbing her purse from the couch on the way. "I know you like to walk in the mornings to get your steps in, so I thought maybe we could leave together? I just need, like, fifteen minutes to get ready."

She looks at her wristwatch, the crease in her brow growing deeper. "You should have scheduled it with me in advance if you wanted to leave together. We're launching the new recovery study at the clinic today and there's a lot to do, so I have to head out now. Next time?"

Ah. The Memory Recovery Study. It's a huge new trial program Sori Clinic is kicking off, the first of its kind, and apparently interest in it has been overwhelming. I saw Mom do an interview about it online the other day and she looked totally confident and collected as she talked about her hopes for the study. "If sounds can erase memories, we believe they also have the potential to restore them," she said. "And if that's possible, we're going to find a way to make it a reality."

She seemed so certain in the video. But she sounded like the exact opposite in the bathroom just now, giving herself a pep talk. I feel like I heard something I shouldn't. Mira Bae? Anxious? Unheard of. I want to ask her about it, how she's really feeling, but she glances at her watch again and I swallow the words.

"Sure. Next time," I say instead. "No problem."

And it really isn't. At least, that's what I tell the whisper of disappointment nudging at the inside of my chest. I should know better than to spring surprise plans on Mom. We haven't lived together since my parents got divorced when I was twelve. She moved to Korea almost immediately after too, which meant I only saw her a couple of times a year when she came to visit, and once when I visited her in Busan. It doesn't take a genius to pick up on the fact that Dr. Bae has priorities. Just because I'm living with her now doesn't mean she's going to change her schedule around for me, especially not when there are big things happening at the clinic. I can be cool about that. Cool and mature.

"I'll send you a Google Calendar invite next time," I say.

"Yena," she sighs.

"What? That wasn't a jab. I'm being genuine! You love Google Calendar."

"Well then, fine, yes, a calendar invite would be very helpful," she says. "I'm sorry I can't be as flexible and spontaneous as your dad, okay?"

There's a sour note to her words that makes me grimace. Why do parents always have to do that? Make it about something it isn't? "How does Dad have anything to do with this?"

"Nothing. I shouldn't have said that." A regretful look passes over her face and she turns toward the door, resting her hand on the doorknob. "Tea tonight? I'll come home a little earlier and we can have an evening snack before bed?" She doesn't look at me when she says it.

"Sure, Mom," I say. I can tell she's trying to extend an olive branch and I take it. It's something. "That sounds good."

With a quick nod, she leaves. A moment later, my phone pings with a calendar invite.

Teatime with Yena (snacks to be provided), 9:00 p.m.

How very Dr. Bae of her. I click accept and head over to the shoe closet.

I swing the doors open, rooting through her impressive collection of footwear. Mom is the kind of person who gets one thing in five different colors if she likes it, which explains why there's an entire catalog of Crocs in here. I push them aside, along with the many pairs of sandals, stilettos, and flats toppling over each other. A rain boot in the corner falls onto its side and a stray mixtape skitters out. Honestly, this woman might be a genius in her field, but at home she's as disorganized as they come.

I grab the tape and stick it into my pocket to take to the clinic. Finally, I find a pair of runners in the corner of the closet. I blow the dust off and try them on. Now that I'm not leaving with Mom, I take my time getting ready, humming to myself as I lace up the shoes. The beginning of a new, committed me. I snap a photo of myself in the shoes and send it to Dad. Who knows, maybe by the end of the summer, I'll be running marathons. I should see if there are any in Busan I can sign up for.

I'm about two minutes into my run when I realize that, actually, running sucks. And running in Korean summer heat? It sucks even more. Even at 8:00 a.m., the humidity is already making me sweat. Maybe it was a bad idea to jog to work. I'm going to be drenched by the time I get there.

But I've already started, bangs clipped back from my forehead, fanny pack clasped around my waist. And more importantly, I already sent that photo to Dad. I can't tell him I quit before I even really began. See, this is why you should never text parents first.

I pause to stick my earphones in and grab the Walkman from my fanny pack. "Where did you get that?" Danielle asked the first time I pulled it out at work. "And do you even know how to use one of those?"

I snapped my fingers, pointing at her. "You said you're a writer, right? Let me guess, you write stand-up comedy. Because that was really funny."

"Your sarcasm, it stings," she said dryly.

"If you're really curious, I got it online after I found out I would be working in the Memotery," I said. "Dr. Bae said the tapes are the heartbeat of the fancy erasure machines they use during the procedure, but when it's in a Walkman, it just plays like a regular tape. I wanted to listen to some."

"Why?"

I shrugged. "I don't know. How can you be surrounded by all these memories and not want to listen to them?"

That was how it had started anyway. A general curiosity about the tapes that filled the shelves. But the more I listened, the more I found a sense of comfort in them, a sense of connection. Not to the people per se, but to the memories themselves, the forgotten ones. It became almost like a mini ritual for me to listen to the sounds and give them one last chance to be remembered in this exact way, this exact combination, before being archived for good.

I pop the Walkman open, expecting to see Patient 1562's tape inside from when I was listening to it yesterday. But it's empty and I remember that I took it out to file it with Danielle. Good thing I have a backup. I reach into my pocket and pull out the cassette tape from the shoe closet, turning it over to look at the spine. Patient 201.

"Thanks for keeping me company, Patient 201," I say, putting it into the Walkman. "You're going to make this run a lot more bearable."

I hit the play button and start running again.

It starts with static. And then wind chimes.

Then the whirring starts. It takes me a moment to place it, but I realize it's the sound of a film reel. For a second, the nostalgia of the sound makes me stumble. It reminds me of the movie days Lucas and I used to have and the time we became obsessed with learning how to use the old film reel machine we found in our Korean school's dusty AV closet. We never did figure that out.

The sounds give way to waves, the lapping of water.

I jog past a playground, an apartment complex, emerging from residential streets into busier ones. Around me people are rushing to catch the bus, walking with their heads bent down to their phones, briefcases and purses bumping against each other as they make their way to work.

It sounds like a lawn mower, the tapping of a knife against a cutting board, a popcorn machine. The waves wash in and out of the background.

Ice cream truck music takes over the soundtrack and a strange feeling begins to creep in as I listen. I turn the corner, jogging through a quieter street lined with coffee shops and restaurants that have yet to open for the day, trying to place the feeling. Why does this all sound so familiar?

And then, a voice.

"Hi, it's me! Meet me at blue hour. You know where."

My heart stops. At least, it feels like it does. It feels like everything in me and around me—my thoughts, my feet, the people passing by—has frozen in time except for the mixtape, playing on unaware. The voice loops again.

"Hi, it's me! Meet me at blue hour. You know where."

And again.

"Meet me at blue hour. You know where."

Not just any voice. *My* voice.

I stagger back, leaning against the wall of a café. My own laughter rings in my ears. The popcorn. The knife. The wind chimes and the film reel and—I inhale sharply. The ice cream truck. *That* ice cream truck. I punch the stop button on the Walkman, rip out my earphones, stuff them into my fanny pack with shaking hands.

What is this? I rack my brain, trying to figure it out. A thought comes to me, an obvious answer, but I push it away almost immediately. There must be some other perfectly reasonable explanation that's not what I'm thinking.

Someone is pulling a terrible prank on me. I'm on a reality TV show. I'm being filmed right now, secretly, forever immortalized in my sweaty, panicked, non-runner-attempting-to-run state.

But the streets are quiet and I'm alone. The realization sinks in.

These are my memories with Lucas, a whole compilation of our friendship sealed in one mixtape. And if this exists, it means that it was used to erase someone's memories.

I remember everything about him. Which means that he erased everything about me.

All the things that felt frozen in the moment suddenly come roaring back. My heartbeat, pounding, my thoughts, clamoring, each one fighting to be heard over the other. One thought rushes to the forefront of my mind. Why? Why would he do that?

And then right behind that thought, another one: Did my mom know about this?

I have to talk to Dr. Bae. Right now.

I start running again, nails digging into my palms. I have to ask her, face-to-face. She knew how devastated I was when Lucas left. How many times did I call her in Korea, crying about it when it happened? How could she keep this from me? Was she the one who conducted the erasure? Does Dad know?

I run harder, shoes pounding against the pavement. My legs are burning and my lungs feel like they're going to burst, but I don't stop. I can see the Sori Clinic building getting closer and I push myself even more. The heat is starting to make my head spin. I'm seeing spots. Someone turns the corner, looking down at their phone, and I'm going too fast to stop in time. I collide right into them, full-body contact like a football player, and fall backward, landing on my side with my elbow skidding against the sidewalk.

I just lie there, stunned. Running was a mistake. A terrible, terrible mistake. Why do people do this to themselves?

"Are you okay?" the person I ran into says in Korean, looking down at me.

I look up. And suddenly, I get it. I'm hallucinating from

the heat. That's it. Because even though he's older and it's been four years since I last saw him, I'd recognize that face anywhere, and there's absolutely no way Lucas Pak is really here, standing right in front of me.

"You're bleeding," he says with a concerned look in his eyes, making me feel like I'm thirteen again.

"Lucas?" I want to say back. But I don't because everyone knows you shouldn't talk to ghosts. So instead, I stumble to my feet, ignoring his outstretched hand and limping as fast as I can into Sori Clinic's building. I press the button for the elevator over and over again until it arrives, taking it up to the twelfth floor.

Joanne, the receptionist, looks up from the front desk and gasps when I enter. "Yena! What happened to you? Your elbow's all bloody! And where'd you get that scratch on your face?"

"Had a bit of an accident on my way to work, but I'm fine," I say. I try to sound breezy, but my voice comes out shakier than I want it to. "I'm just going to get cleaned up. And, um, could you tell Dr. Bae to come find me in the Memotery when you see her?"

"Sure," Joanne says, looking worried.

I limp to the bathroom, pausing at the window to look down at the sidewalk. Lucas is gone. But of course, he was never there to begin with. The mixtape is overworking my imagination, making me see him where he isn't.

The mixtape. I need to get to the bottom of that. I shake my head and continue on, but even though I know it wasn't real, I can't get his face out of my mind.

Lucas Pak, the best friend who left me. The boy who erased me.

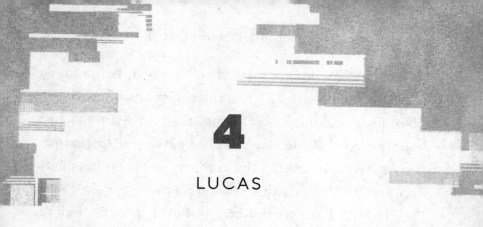

4

LUCAS

I watch the girl limp away, blood dripping from her elbow, and I think about chasing after her to make sure she's okay. I can still feel the impact of our collision, and I didn't even fall down. I can't imagine how much worse it must have been for her.

She disappears into a building, but I still stare at the spot where she stood. The way she looked at me burns in my mind. She had pretty eyes, dark and fox-like, but it was the emotion in them that made it hard to look away. I couldn't quite read it, but there was something there, something vulnerable. She didn't seem to want my help though. I couldn't help but feel a little disappointed when she rushed off without a word.

Then again, I wouldn't want to talk to the guy who was too busy looking at his phone to watch where he's going either.

"Smooth," I mutter to myself.

I step to the side and look down at my phone again, zooming in on Sori Clinic's location on Naver Maps. It should be around here somewhere. But first, I duck into a 7-Eleven and pick up a small travel-size box of bandages. Not because I think I'll run into that girl again. It's just always a good idea to have some first aid on you. Just in case.

As I'm about to leave the store, my phone buzzes in my pocket. It's Umma, calling me on Kakao.

"Hello?" I answer in Korean, shuffling to the back of the store, where there are a few tables set up. A couple sits at one of them, sharing a triangle kimbap and a carton of banana milk, but otherwise it's empty. I pull out a chair and take a seat. Conversations with Umma always run longer than not.

"Lucas, hi! How's Korea so far? Are you with Harabeoji?"

"Um . . ." My parents, like Harabeoji, have no idea what my plan with Sori Clinic's Memory Recovery Study is. No one knows. And as far as I'm concerned, they don't need to know yet. I don't want to worry anyone or get their hopes up before anything has even happened.

"He's with his caretaker today," I say, switching to English. I speak in a mix of both languages with my parents, like I do with Harabeoji. "So I'm just out exploring Busan by myself for a bit."

Not a lie. After breakfast this morning, a woman named Mrs. Cha came to spend the day with him. "This is my grandson, Lucas," Harabeoji introduced me with a proud pat on the shoulder. "He's visiting me from . . ."

His voice trailed off, his lips pulling down into a frown.

I could almost see him searching for the word inside his head, slipping through his fingers and evading his grasp. "From . . ."

"Canada," I said. "Edmonton, Canada."

"Oh yes. Edmonton. Canada." He nodded. "He's visiting me from Canada."

Samchon said Harabeoji was having a good day yesterday. It's enough for me to almost forget that things are different now, that they're going to keep on being different if we don't do anything about it. But even from my brief interactions with him this morning, I could tell that not every day is a good day.

"Well, remember, if Harabeoji's too busy and you want to come home earlier, just say the word," Umma says on the phone. "We miss you at the restaurant."

"Umma, I literally just got here yesterday."

"I'm just saying."

I sigh, guilt churning in the pit of my stomach. My parents weren't too keen on the idea of me going to Korea for the whole summer. It took some convincing to get them on board, one of the biggest reasons being that they'd lose a set of hands at the family restaurant. I've been working at Lim's Kitchen ever since they opened in Edmonton, becoming one of the most popular mom-and-pop Korean restaurants in town, and I know how much they rely on me there. Even before that, when we lived in Vancouver and ran a restaurant by the same name, I was helping out wherever I could. Well. Almost wherever.

"When I get back, can we finally talk about me joining the kitchen?" I ask.

I can feel Umma's hesitation through the phone. "I thought you were happy serving food. Why do you want to cook it too?"

"I told you, I like cooking. And I'm good at it. Harabeoji's taught me a lot over the years."

"Cooking at home with your grandpa is one thing, but a restaurant is totally different," she says. "You've seen how many burns I've gotten from the kitchen. It's too stressful and not the safest for you. You're still too young. Besides, we need you as a server and on the administrative end of things. That's already helping a lot."

We've had this same conversation a hundred times already. It's not that I mind being a server or taking care of admin. But when I think about the restaurant, nothing is as exciting to me as being at the stove, testing out new recipes, and creating the dishes myself. The kitchen is the place where I've been most keen to help out and the place that Umma and Appa seem the most adamant about keeping me away from, insisting that I'm not ready yet.

"You said we could at least talk about it after I graduate," I remind her.

"I mean . . ." She trails off. "Okay, fine. We can discuss it when you're back. Now tell me how things are going over there."

I can tell by how quickly she changes the subject that she probably doesn't plan on discussing it at all. But I bite my tongue and let it go for now. I'll bring it up again when I'm back.

"It's been really nice to see Harabeoji again," I say. "Samchon too."

Her voice softens. "I'm glad. I just hope it won't be too hard on you with his health being what it is."

I want to ask if it's been hard for her too. Harabeoji is her dad, after all, but we've never talked about it. Before I can ask, she says, "I got your menu updates. It looks good."

"Oh. Yeah? More modern, right?"

"Yeah. But I think we should change one or two things . . ."

As expected, the call stretches on for a while. I take notes on all the changes she wants, jotting them down on the back of a napkin. Then, before we say goodbye, she runs through a string of final reminders for me.

"Make sure you're eating three meals a day. Drink lots of water to stay hydrated. It's hot there, right? And humid? Don't stay out too late either and be back at Samchon's before dark. And don't follow any strangers anywhere. There are weird people in the world."

Every conversation with Umma ends with some kind of reiteration of this warning list. I've heard it so many times, I could probably write an entire book about it.

"Umma, I'm eighteen," I sigh. "I'll be fine."

"That's still young to be so far away from us," she says.

That was the second biggest reason my parents didn't want me to go to Korea and why Samchon was surprised they agreed to it at all. Before this trip, I'd never spent a night apart from them, and it nearly made them sick with worry to think about what might happen to me without them. Honestly, the humidity in Korea might be a lot, but it's a breath of fresh air compared to how suffocated I feel sometimes being under their constant watch.

"Your dad and I just want you to be safe so you can have a good time," she says.

I instantly feel bad for what I was thinking. They're only doing their best to look out for me. I should be grateful for that.

"Thanks, Umma. I'll be safe."

We hang up. I sit at the table for a moment longer, staring at my napkin of restaurant notes. For as much time as we spend talking, I can't help but feel like neither of us has actually said a whole lot.

I fold up the napkin, tuck it into my pocket, and head out of 7-Eleven.

Sori Clinic is on the twelfth floor of a tall concrete building. The same one, I realize, that the girl I collided with earlier went into. There's a receptionist sitting behind the front desk, a Korean woman maybe in her early thirties, dressed in a smart navy blazer, brown hair with one light blonde strand in the front framing her face in perfect curtain bangs. Everything from her image to the sparkling white countertop, the cushioned mahogany chairs lined up in the waiting room, all full, with neatly stacked magazines resting on low glass coffee tables, feels intentional and meticulously designed. I suddenly feel self-conscious in my jeans and T-shirt.

"Welcome to Sori of Us Clinic, how may I help you?" the receptionist says in Korean. Her name tag says Joanne Kim, and underneath that "Korean / English." I read on Sori Clinic's website that they run on an entirely bilingual system and can offer translation services in other languages if requested. From what the website suggested, it seems like they've recently started gaining more recognition outside of Korea, with people traveling from all over the world specifically to see them. A quick sweep of the people in the waiting room tells me that this is probably true—it looks like an equal mix of foreigners and local Koreans. In fact, the waiting room is filled to the brim, abuzz with a combination of excited and nervous energy. They must be doing really well here.

"Hi," I say in English, hurriedly approaching the front desk. "I'm here to talk to someone about the Memory Recovery Study."

"Are you a participant or the companion of a participant?" Joanne asks, seamlessly switching languages to match me. Her fingers are already poised over her computer keyboard, waiting to search me up.

"Neither yet," I say. "I'm here to see if any spots have opened up for the summer."

"Ah." She folds her hands together, lowering them in her lap. "Unfortunately, our program is already quite full. If there are any openings, we'll definitely post it on our website, but in the meantime, you can join our online waitlist for any updates."

Her gaze is already moving past me toward the person standing behind me in line. I take a deep breath, channel my inner Harabeoji. "Always follow up with questions," he'd say to me whenever a vendor didn't have what we needed for the restaurant. "If there's something you need, try to end the conversation with a plan instead of a no."

Harabeoji was the owner and head cook of the original Lim's Kitchen in Korea. He gave my parents everything they needed in order to launch the restaurant in Canada, but it was me who he treated like an apprentice, who he shared all his stories and insider tips with.

"People are everything," he'd say, rolling me an egg across the counter where he was teaching me how to make his famous gyeran jjim. I was twelve, hanging on to his every word, catching the egg before it could slip to the floor. "You want them to remember you. That goes for vendors, business partners, customers. So how can you make sure they think of you first when the opportunity arises? You don't just wait for them to come to you. You leave a door open for them."

I picture Harabeoji in my mind's eye, his crooked smile, his weathered hands, the burns on his arms from years of cooking. He was always so good at opening closed doors, a trait I did not naturally inherit. I resist the temptation to end the conversation with an "Okay, thank you very much" and press on. *You came prepared for this*, I remind myself. *You have a plan.*

"Is there a doctor I can speak to in the meantime about the program?" I ask.

Joanne shakes her head. "Because the program is already full, our doctors are currently only taking consultations regarding the erasure procedure."

"I understand. I'm actually also interested in that. Would I be able to book a consultation while I'm here?"

I'm not interested at all, really, but if I make a consultation for an erasure, maybe I can get more insight into the recovery study in the process. It's not a rock-solid plan, but it's an open door.

"Sure," Joanne says, typing something on her computer. "Let's see here . . . We have an opening three weeks from now on Thursday if that works for you?"

Three weeks from now? My heart sinks. So much for my open-door plan. My trip will be nearly half over by then. There's got to be something I can do to make this move faster.

I take a breath. Okay. It's fine. I'm still on the waitlist. I'll come back every day to be first in line for an available opening, twice a day if I have to. Just as I'm thanking Joanne for her time, I catch a glimpse of someone in the corner of my eye. I do a double take. It's the girl from the street, walking down the hallway across the room, holding a big cardboard box. I knew she went into this building, but I didn't think we'd cross paths again, especially not here. She disappears behind a wall, vanishing from my sight.

"Sorry, I'll actually pass on the appointment for now, but is there a bathroom I can use here?" I ask Joanne.

Joanne points me down the hall and I walk in that direction. But instead of going to the bathroom, I do a quick check behind my shoulder to make sure no one is watching, and then I turn the corner in the direction the girl went.

I don't know what compels me to do it. But I can still see her eyes in my mind, the way she looked at me, the pull I felt toward her. I feel like I've seen her somewhere before, or maybe not, maybe she just has one of those faces. I'm not sure. I just know I want to see her again, to make sure she's okay.

Don't follow any strangers anywhere, Umma's voice echoes in my head. I push it away. This doesn't count.

I quicken my pace and for the second time today, I run right into someone turning the corner.

Or at least, I almost do. The woman in front of me startles and jumps back before we fully collide. "Oh goodness, I'm so sorry! Didn't see you there," she says in English.

"No, I'm sorry, it's my fault," I say, bowing my head in apology.

I straighten up. She takes a look at my face and the polite smile she was wearing a moment ago flickers into an expression of surprise.

Ah, shoot. She probably realizes that I'm not supposed to be here. Judging by the clipboard in her hands and the name tag clipped to her shirt, she definitely works here. I do a double take at her name tag. *Dr. Mira Bae.* Where have I heard that name before?

Of course. It was all over Sori Clinic's website. She's the founder and head of the company.

My mind immediately goes into overdrive. This could be good. Lucky, even. I've just found myself in the audience of the most knowledgeable, powerful person in the clinic. There has to be something I can do to work this to my advantage. *Open door.*

But I'm not quick enough. She masks her surprise into a more neutral, professional expression and says, "Can I help with you anything? It's typically employees only back here."

There's a coolness and finality to her voice that makes

me flounder, like she knows I have no business being here and she knows I know it too. She looks at me carefully, as if trying to read my next move.

"Um . . . I was just . . . looking for the bathroom," I say.

I can almost hear the door slam shut in my mind.

She nods slowly, guiding me back down the hall where I came from and pointing me to the bathroom. "It's right over there."

"Thanks. I must have missed it."

She smiles in a way that's meant to be reassuring, but there's still something in her eyes, a wariness almost nearing suspicion, that makes me feel less than comforted. I wasn't even doing anything that bad, but I can't help but feel guilty under her watchful gaze. I bow my head one more time and duck into the bathroom.

When I come back out a moment later, she's still standing in the hallway, chatting to an employee. She locks her eyes on mine, gives me a smile, says, "Have a good day."

"Thanks. You too," I say.

I can feel her watching me as I hurry out the clinic's front doors. Dr. Bae must take the security at her clinic really seriously. Makes sense, I guess. It's sensitive work they do here. I better be careful when I come back so they don't think I'm some kind of weirdo.

I take the stairs down, too antsy to wait for the elevator. Well, that was a total fail.

The box of bandages bumps against my leg through the pocket of my jeans. I'll have to think of a better strategy for tomorrow. Not only to find out more at the clinic, but to maybe get a glimpse of the girl with the pretty eyes again. I keep my chin up, bounding down the rest of the stairs.

SOUND

THE KNIFE AND THE CUTTING BOARD
12 YEARS OLD

We told you, didn't we? We said kids shouldn't play with knives. Someone could get hurt.

It was evening. The boy's parents were working late and the girl had nowhere to go. Her father was on a date and her mother had just moved across the sea, so to the boy's house she went, where his grandfather was asleep in the armchair in front of the couch, the TV still playing reruns on the Food Network.

They were doing homework, or rather the boy was doing homework while the girl thumbed through a textbook, looking bored. Her stomach growled. Noticing, he asked, "Do you want some food? Or should we finish our homework first?"

She immediately slammed the textbook closed. "All done! What should we eat?"

She followed him to the kitchen cupboards, where he rummaged around, pulled out a can of Spam. "How's kimchi fried rice with Spam?"

"I would never say no to that! Top three favorite foods

of all time. How can I help?"

"You don't have to. It's easy."

"I want to." Her eyes landed on us, lighting up. "I can chop things?"

"Okay. Want to cut up the Spam, then? Bite-size pieces."

She saluted. "Yes, Chef."

He smiled, glancing at the living room, where his grandpa was sleeping. "Just don't tell my parents. They don't like it when I use the stove. Harabeoji showed me how to use it safely and he's right there if anything goes wrong, so we'll be okay."

They got to work, the boy searching the fridge for day-old rice and kimchi, the girl tearing off the lid of the Spam can. We could tell by the way she looked at us that despite the confidence in her voice she was a little uncertain, perhaps not used to handling something so sharp. But she went for it anyway, grabbing the handle of me, the knife, and plopping the brick of meat onto me, the board. From the start it felt unceremonious and awkward.

"You okay with that?" the boy's voice called from inside the fridge.

"Yeah. This is fun actually. Mom never let me touch anything in the kitchen."

"It's been a couple weeks now since she left, right?"

"Yeah." Her chopping was clumsy and erratic. Was this what being seasick felt like? We felt like we were getting a headache.

"Must be weird."

"Not really. She and Dad have been separated for over a year. Now the divorce is just official."

"I mean the fact that she's so far away."

"Oh. Yeah."

Chop chop chop. Her movements got even more brash. How could we get off this ride?

"I know last week you were crying at Korean school . . ." The boy's voice was careful, much like how we wished the girl would be in handling us.

"Oh, that? Don't worry, I'm over it. It's nothing."

We could tell by the way her hand started shaking that it probably wasn't nothing and she probably wasn't over it. We really started to feel unsteady now.

"Are you sure?"

"Yeah. I'm really—ouch!"

We didn't do it on purpose, honest. It just happened. She let me, the knife, clatter against me, the board, as the blade sliced her finger. She pulled back, blood on her skin.

The boy came running. "What happened?"

"Sorry. It just slipped."

"Don't be sorry. Wait right here."

He dug around in the drawers, found a box of bandages and carefully unpeeled one, sticking it around the girl's finger. She watched him quietly as he worked.

"Better?" he said.

She shook her head and said in a small voice, "No. I miss my mom."

His face softened and he stepped forward, putting his arms around her. "I'll finish the rice," he said.

We felt safer in his hands. He cut up the Spam, the kimchi, turned on the stove, fried it together with the cold rice, adding sesame oil, sesame seeds, a dash of green onions. He fried two eggs too, sunny side up, and laid them neatly on top of the plates of rice.

They ate in silence, not talking about the mother anymore, the girl only breaking it once to hold up her bandaged finger and say with a smile, "Hey, I just realized. My first kitchen wound. That makes me a chef like you, right?"

He laughed and then they settled back into silence. But the quiet wasn't awkward. It was familiar. It reminded us of how we are with each other, me, the knife, and me, the board. Comfortable and without a need for words.

5

YENA

"Um. What happened to you and what are you doing with the laptop?"

I imagine myself in that moment as Danielle sees me, walking into her shift with her tumbler of black coffee in hand, squinting to confirm that that is indeed her coworker crouched in the corner of the Memotery and not some gremlin that's broken into the office. I all but hiss at the light as she opens the door and lets it fall shut again.

"Important personal research, if you must know," I say. I clear my throat. "Actually, now that you're here, would you mind telling me the password for the laptop? I've been trying to get in for the past twenty minutes."

"You haven't answered the first part." She gestures toward my elbows, hastily bandaged and speckled with a few spots of dried blood that I missed while cleaning myself up. "Did a box of tapes fall on you?"

"I jogged to work today and ran into someone outside," I say.

The image of Lucas's face flickers through my mind.

It really looked just like him, down to the light freckles scattered across his cheekbones, the serious arch of his eyebrows that always made him look like he was lost in thought. Older, of course, than when I last saw him, and taller too. Cruel of my brain to play tricks on me like that. This is all because of the mixtape.

I can still hear the sound of the popcorn machine, the waves and the film reel, my own voice echoing back at me. And the music from that damn ice cream truck that I'm trying my hardest to ignore. Sori Clinic has been extra busy since I got here, and I've been helping wherever an extra pair of hands was needed all morning. But as soon as I got the chance to slip away to the Memotery, I grabbed the laptop to try to find information on Lucas's file. I hold the computer out to Danielle now, a hopeful look on my face.

"So about that password?" I say.

"Looks like you locked yourself out for too many wrong attempts," Danielle says, taking the laptop from me with a shake of her head. "What personal research are you doing anyway?"

Danielle wouldn't care. Why would she? I'm not her friend, I'm her archive assistant and she can barely tolerate that. Besides, she doesn't know a thing about me and Lucas. But I feel like I'm driving myself mad trying to understand what I heard, and the words come tumbling out of my mouth before I can stop them.

"I had this childhood best friend who suddenly moved

away and stopped talking to me one day. I never knew why, but today I found a mixtape of our memories together, which leads me to believe that he didn't just stop talking to me; he might have actually erased me altogether. But . . . that would be unhinged, right? Like why would he do that? And does that mean my mom knew about it? Because there's nothing, and I mean nothing, that happens in this clinic that she doesn't know about. So was she just, I don't know, never going to tell me? Was that her plan? Hide the tape in a rain boot and hope I'd never find out? Well, surprise, surprise, even Dr. Bae makes mistakes because look where we are now!"

I'm breathing hard and Danielle is staring at me with a stunned expression. I think she's going to tell me to calm the hell down and get back to work. But then there's a shift in her face, something like a softening, an unspoken understanding. Wordlessly, she types something into the laptop and hands it over.

"Put in the patient number and the file should come up," she says. "We have limited access so we can't see everything in the system, but you'll be able to see the name of the patient and the date they got their erasure."

Her help catches me so off guard that tears prick at the corners of my eyes.

"Thanks," I say, voice cracking.

She simply nods and sits down next to me on the floor as I type into the computer: *Patient 201.*

It takes less than a second for the information to appear

on-screen. My eyes scan the words once, twice, a third time. And there it is, confirming what I already knew, once, twice, a third time. Any doubt I'd had that this was all in my head comes to a screeching halt. I should be relieved, really. I can say that I know what I heard, that I can trust myself.

But all I feel in my gut is a deep, sinking, churning feeling, as if I'm being swallowed up from the inside out.

Patient 201: Lucas Pak.

I look at the date. It's been nearly four years since he erased me. Exactly when he disappeared from my life.

"I'm sorry, Yena," Danielle says, her voice somber. "I know how shitty it is to be forgotten."

When I look up at her, there's sympathy in her eyes, but there's also an undercurrent of something darker, angrier. I'm about to ask if she's gone through a similar thing when she blinks and the look is gone. She pats me on the shoulder, standing.

"Want to get your mind off it? These tapes aren't going to organize themselves."

"Sure," I say, because what else is there for me to do? Danielle is already back to business, going through the day's boxes. Even if I wanted to talk more about this, I don't know what I'd say. I don't even know what to think. "Let's do that."

Dad's phone has been going to voicemail all day. He hasn't even seen the running photo I sent him this morning according to his read receipts, but honestly, maybe that's a good thing. I don't plan on ever doing it again after the disaster that was today, and the last thing I need is another disappointed conversation on how I never stick to things. After my tenth failed call, I send him a text message.

Me:

Call me back please, your one and only daughter is having a crisis.

Me:

SOS, emergency, 911, or 119 in Korea, etc., etc.

Me:

(I'm safe though btw so don't actually call 911.)

Somehow, I made it through my shift and then I squeezed through all the people milling around Sori Clinic and dragged myself home. By the time I got off, the clinic was absolutely packed, even more than it was this morning. It was three times as busy as it usually is, which I assume is because of the new study. The crowd in the lobby was as restless as I felt inside, murmuring about the frustrating wait times, the heat, the stuffiness in the staircase where they were spilling out in what was most certainly a fire hazard. There were even people waiting outside the building just trying to get inside.

As soon as I got back to the apartment, I threw Mom's cursed running shoes into my empty suitcase, locking it shut and shoving it under my bed. There. I never want to even think about running again. Then I showered, blasting cold water over my body, scrubbing myself clean of dried sweat and blood. But the restless coil still tightened in my chest.

I wanted to talk about it. But Dad is MIA and there are still hours before my scheduled teatime with Dr. Bae, who never did end up coming to find me in the Memotery today despite my request to Joanne.

So here I am now, damp hair wrapped in a towel, sitting on the couch in a pair of pajama shorts and an oversize T-shirt, staring at my phone.

Who can I talk to? Who would understand? Are my closest friends really my *dad* and my supervisor at work? Not that five minutes of listening to my mental breakdown and taking pity on me counts as friendship exactly. I try not to dwell on that too much, otherwise I will, in fact, simply fade out of existence from embarrassment.

I scroll through my Instagram. Familiar faces flash through my feed. Cindy from English 12 who was always fun to work on projects with, traveling through Europe with her friends, a last hurrah before they all go off to different universities and colleges in the fall. Marty, the friend of a friend who I met at a party once, volunteering at the local hospital. I remember them telling me that their dream is to be a doctor, how impressed they were when I said my mom is the founder of Sori Clinic.

"Are you serious? She's a legend," they exclaimed. "That must be so cool, getting a front-row seat to all the developments in memory erasing. Honestly, it still seems like the stuff out of movies to me, but it's probably just regular dinner conversation for you."

I remember laughing along, nodding, not bothering to correct them by saying I only have dinner with my mom once or twice a year when she visits, and most of that time is spent with her worrying about my life going to waste.

Maybe she wasn't wrong to worry. Look at everyone else, going on adventures, working toward their dreams. And me?

I'm sitting here, still frozen in something that happened years ago.

My phone rings. It's Mom.

I take a deep breath, answering. "Hello?"

"Hi, Yena. I'm so sorry, but I'm going to have to reschedule our teatime. You saw how wild things are here today, right? So many people showing up unannounced, trying to get into the study even though it's full. And don't even get me started on all the technical errors slowing us down on the back end. Anyway, it's been a far messier day than I'd hoped. I'm going to have to stay extra late tonight to try and get us back on track."

Why am I not surprised? And if I'm not surprised, why

do I still feel disappointed?

"Yena? Are you there?" she says after I'm quiet for a moment too long.

"Yeah. I'm here."

"I'm sorry. I really didn't want to cancel. I heard you were looking for me at the office today too, but I didn't get a chance to swing by the Archive. Did you need to talk to me about something?"

This is my chance. I open my mouth to speak but nothing comes out. Maybe it's because I can hear the stress laced in her voice. I want to tell her it's fine. I want to tell her, well, actually it's not. I want to tell her I found Lucas's mixtape. I have so many questions, so many feelings I don't know how to feel. I've been waiting all day to talk to her, but this isn't a conversation I want to have on the phone, especially not when she has one foot out the door.

"It's cool. You do your thing," I say.

"I'll make it up to you," she promises.

"I take cash," I joke, but it comes out flat.

We hang up and as I sit there alone, the feeling from earlier comes back stronger than ever, that while the world is moving on and taking care of its business, I've somehow been left behind. The heaviness of it is overwhelming.

"It doesn't matter. Nothing matters," I remind myself out loud. "That's just how things are. There's no point holding on too tight when everything changes eventually." *When everyone leaves eventually.*

The reminder helps, a little, enough for me to push the feelings aside and turn on the TV. I put on *Mean Girls*, my comfort movie, and let it play, laughing at every right moment until I've all but forgotten the heaviness inside.

It's my day off, but God bless Joanne for asking me to come into the clinic for a couple of hours to help out because I would 100 percent be spending the whole day wallowing in bed if she didn't.

"I'm sorry," she said over the phone. "You should be out there enjoying Busan on your day off."

Honestly, I feel like I haven't seen much of Busan at all since I arrived. I've mostly been at home or at Sori Clinic. It's not that I don't want to explore more or that I haven't had the time, I just don't know where to start. And maybe a part of me is also a little nervous about wandering around an unknown city by myself.

"Happy to do it," I told Joanne.

But as I near the clinic, I see the crowd of people waiting outside the building like they were when I left work yesterday, only it's gotten even bigger. I wonder how many of them have actually been admitted into the program and how many are here to try to grab any available opening. It's a big mix of people, but the majority of them are elderly folks accompanied by sons, daughters, grandchildren. There are reporters here today as well, microphones and cameras, passersby staring in curiosity.

Mom wasn't kidding when she said it was a mess. How am I supposed to get through all this?

I squeeze through the crowd and somehow get into the building despite the grumblings of "Hey, no cutting!" behind me.

Tony Han-Larson, thirtysomething and one of Dr. Bae's assistants at the clinic, who moved all the way from England to work here, is standing in the first-floor lobby with a clipboard, looking beside himself with stress. This was maybe not quite what he had in mind when he took the job. He's so tall, his buzz cut pokes out above the crowd, making him easy to spot.

"Yena," he says when I make my way over to him. He pulls a name tag out of his pocket, tangled up in a lanyard. It says STAFF across it in bold letters. "Do you have one of these already? If not, put this on. No one will give you trouble for passing them if you have this."

"Thank you." I don't usually wear a name tag at work since I'm just in the Memotery, but today I gratefully put the lanyard around my neck. I look around the packed lobby. "I can't believe how many people are here. I thought it would have calmed down after the first day, but it only seems busier."

"I know. I mean, I think we all knew there would be a lot of interest in the Memory Recovery Study, but we didn't expect so many people to show up just to try and get on a waitlist. Dr. Bae did a few prerecorded television interviews that'll be airing throughout this week, so we should be prepared for this to continue as more people hear about the study." He shakes his head. "Crowd management was not in my job description."

"I hope this doesn't make me sound like a terrible person, but could we tell them to go home?" I ask. "This could be an email. We can set up some kind of online waitlist for people to sign up on instead, can't we?"

"Already set up and communicated to people. But they seem to think that showing up in person with their family member suffering from dementia will help their chances of getting into the study faster." He sighs, lowering his voice. "I'm not going to lie, it's working. I've let more people upstairs than I should. Joanne is furious with me."

I wince. "Best of luck to you withstanding Joanne's fury. What can I do to help?"

"If you're up for the task, can you bring down the water bottles from the clinic and pass them out to people waiting outside? It's a hot day and there are a lot of elderly folks out there."

"Yes, sir," I say.

For the next hour, I take the elevator up and down from the clinic, carrying down water bottles and passing them out. Slowly, the crowd thins as people either give up waiting or decide to take Tony's advice to register for the waitlist online. The few people who actually do have a spot in the study already are filtered through the line and sent upstairs.

By the time I'm making my fifth trip down to the lobby with my arms full of water bottles, I'm starting to feel like maybe we've got a handle on this situation. Lucky for me because I'm pretty sure my arms are going to fall off from all this heavy lifting.

The elevator doors open and before I can step out, I see him.

The light dusting of freckles on his nose, the eyebrows turned in thought.

It's the boy from yesterday, talking to Tony. And just like yesterday, he looks exactly as I remember Lucas Pak to be.

Is my mind playing tricks on me again? I close my eyes, count to three, open them again. He's still there, talking to Tony.

"If you've already signed up for the online waitlist, that's really the best you can do right now," Tony is saying in English.

"Could I leave my contact information with you as well? My name is Lucas Pak. My grandfather's name is Lim Hanpyo. He has Alzheimer's and this study would be invaluable for him."

Lucas Pak. The elevator doors are about to slide shut and I quickly shuffle out, leaving the water bottles by the door. Tony is taking notes on his clipboard and nodding.

"All right. I have your information, but again, waiting to hear back about the waitlist is probably your best bet," he says.

Lucas nods, a disappointed slump in his shoulders. "Thank you," he says, and then he walks away.

For a moment, I'm frozen. *Lucas Pak. He said his name is Lucas Pak.* And then I move. I can't help myself. Almost as if I'm in a trance, I run after him, out of the lobby and onto the street, until his back is right in front of me.

"Lucas?" I say.

He stops and turns at the sound of his name. For a second, his eyes widen in recognition and a million thoughts fly through my head.

He knows me. He remembers me. I've imagined our reunion so many times, but I would never have guessed it would be like this, here in Korea, under such strange circumstances. I've thought about what I would say, how I would say it, and in every single iteration I was the cool girl who's moved on. *Lucas, right? Oh my god, it's been so long. I almost didn't recognize you!*

In none of my imaginings did I think I would be the one standing in front of him, holding my breath to see if he could even recall my name.

"Hi," I say, heart pounding in my chest. "Remember me?"

"You're the girl from yesterday," he says. Unlike when he asked me if I was okay yesterday, he speaks in English this time, matching me. "The runner."

I feel like someone's struck me. *You can't be disappointed if you knew,* a voice in my head says. But knowing something and colliding with it headfirst are two different things.

"That's me," I say, quickly covering the shock on my face with a smile. "How are you? I mean, after the run-in yesterday. Sorry about that, by the way."

"Me? I'm fine. What about you? You're the one who had that nasty fall."

"I'm okay. Thanks for asking."

He smiles a small smile back. "Good."

"Yeah. Good."

Silence falls between us. His eyes start to wander away, like he wants to leave this conversation with a stranger. I don't want him to leave. I don't want him to think I'm a stranger.

Before I can say anything else, he looks at me again and says, "How did you know my name?"

Uh-oh. What do I say? "I overheard you talking to Tony." Not a lie. I hold up my name tag. "I'm, uh, I work here."

"I see. And what's your name?"

"Yena. Yena Bae."

I watch his face for a reaction, for any sign of familiarity, but he simply nods. "Yena Bae. Here."

He reaches into his pocket, pulls out a small box, tosses it to me. I catch it, turning it over in my hands. It's a travel-size pack of bandages.

"In case you have any more running accidents," he says. His voice is serious but there's humor in his eyes. It's so nostalgic, I feel a physical ache in my chest.

I don't know how to say any of the things I really want

to. I want to ask him why he erased me, but of course I can't do that. He doesn't know why, at least not anymore. He couldn't answer even if he wanted to.

He's raising his hand in a wave goodbye. I should let it go. I should let him go. There's no point holding on, no matter how much I feel like my heart is going to burst if I don't. But when I open my mouth, it's not a goodbye that comes out. I hear myself say, "I can help you get into the Memory Recovery Study."

Surprise crosses his face. "What?"

"I heard you say your grandfather has Alzheimer's. I can help you get him into the study. I mean, I can't promise anything. But it sounds like he's important to you and if there's anything I can do to help, I'll try." I hold up the bandages. "You know. As a thank-you."

"That's really nice of you," he says slowly, as if unsure whether I'm telling the truth.

"Maybe we can exchange numbers and I'll call you about it," I say.

At first, I think he's going to say no. I would if I were him. But I heard the desperation in his voice when he was talking to Tony, and I see it in his eyes now, battling with the skepticism of accepting an offer from a stranger. The desperation wins. He pulls out his phone. "Okay. Let's do that," he says.

We do and I can't help but feel my emotions tangle with each other all the more, complicated and strange. But in the midst of everything—the hurt, the confusion, the sense of betrayal I haven't been able to shake since finding his mixtape—there's something like determination. I always wondered why I was the one who was left behind, and now, even if he can't explain it to me straight on, I have a chance to talk to him again, to potentially figure things out another way.

I may have felt frozen in time, but now it feels like the ice around me is starting to crack. And I won't let this chance slip away.

6

LUCAS

When I get back to Samchon's place, Harabeoji is watching the news on TV. I'm feeling pretty good, hopeful even, after meeting Yena Bae. I was hoping I'd see her again, but I didn't think it would happen quite like this. I replay our conversation in my head. I don't know how I got so lucky as to earn her help and a part of me wonders if I should have been more wary about accepting it, but a good offer is a good offer. I'm not about to let it pass me by.

I'm still thinking about her as I greet Harabeoji and Mrs. Cha, who's making tea in the kitchen. After hearing Yena speak, I decide that her voice is even prettier than her eyes.

"Ugh," Harabeoji says, lifting the remote control. "Why are people so interested in stuff like this? I don't get it."

I follow his gaze to the TV screen. They're reporting on Sori Clinic and the huge crowd that turned up for the Memory Recovery Study. My stomach flips. Am I in one of these shots? Luckily, the screen cuts just in time to a video clip of Dr. Mira Bae explaining the study. She looks exactly like she does in person: professional and polished, with an air of measured confidence.

"Consider the implications of restoring memories through our existing sound technology. Life-changing would be an understatement, no?" she says. "We are on the brink of new discoveries, and I couldn't be more excited to see where this study will take us."

"You don't think it's interesting?" I say to Harabeoji, trying to keep my voice casual.

"Interesting? It's absurd," he says. "You don't play around with people's memories."

"But you said so yourself just the other day, technology is amazing," I say. "Remember how you were able to watch the livestream of my graduation?"

Harabeoji looks at me as if I've grown two heads. "Ya, are those two things the same? A livestream and going into someone's memories? It's unnatural to tamper with your brain like that."

An uneasy feeling begins to unfurl in my stomach. I purposely kept my plan from Harabeoji because I didn't want him to get his hopes up in case it didn't work out, but I didn't even consider the fact that he might be completely against it. I know memory tampering is controversial, but with his condition, how could he not see the benefits of at least trying everything he can to get better?

"What if they can give you a cure?" I press. "Isn't that invaluable?"

"Sure, but I don't think I'd trust people who are experts in erasing memories to be the ones to find it." He turns the TV off and the screen goes blank. "Just because they can make things disappear doesn't mean they can bring things back."

Mrs. Cha carries out a tray of omija cha, iced for the hot summer day, setting it on the coffee table. The earlier hopeful feeling I had when I first came through the door evaporates. Even with Yena's help, how am I supposed to convince Harabeoji that this is the right choice for him? The only choice?

I sit next to Harabeoji, sipping the iced tea with him and Mrs. Cha, only half listening as she fills me in on what they got up to this morning. I'm still lost in my thoughts on how to convince Harabeoji to change his mind as she clears our empty cups away and invites me to join them on their afternoon walk.

"Your mom called, by the way," Harabeoji says as I follow him to his room so he can get ready. "She's worried about the restaurant."

"She's always worried about the restaurant," I say. She's already sent me nine messages about it today and counting. It's a bit concerning how her messages come in at all hours of the day considering the time difference. Makes me wonder when she sleeps.

"Restaurants are hard work," he says, reaching into his closet and pulling out a fleece jacket. "Did you know I used to run one?"

I still. "Yes. Of course. The original Lim's Kitchen."

"I was quite famous, you know." He puts on the jacket, zipping it all the way up to his chin. "Especially my gyeran jjim. No one could steam eggs like me. I'll tell you about it sometime."

An image of a younger Harabeoji rolling an egg across the table to me flashes through my mind. I've held on to every recipe he's taught me, every life lesson. *People are everything. You want them to remember you.* But what's the point of people remembering you if you can't even remember yourself?

"Sure," I say, a lump in my throat. "I'd like that. Now let's get you into something cooler for our walk. It's hot today."

He looks down at his jacket, looking confused as to why he put that on. I help him change into a lighter summer vest and we leave his bedroom. I expect him to put on his shoes like Mrs. Cha is already doing, but instead, he turns into the living room and sits on the couch.

"Harabeoji?" I say.

"Hmm?"

"Aren't we going on a walk?"

"In a minute. Mrs. Cha is going to make us tea first."

I open my mouth, but no words come out. I don't know what to say. Mrs. Cha must sense this because she puts a gentle hand on my shoulder and then goes over to the couch to help Harabeoji to his feet.

"We already had tea. It's time to stretch our legs now," she says.

The words are still stuck in my throat as we head outside together. I wish I knew the right way to respond, but the only thing I can think of in the moment is that I have to fix this. No matter what, I have to make him see that the recovery study is our only chance to save him. I might not have the words, but I hold on to that determination as tight as I can.

* * *

Yena:

Hi, it's Yena Bae. Would you like to grab a coffee with me today?

Yena:

I have some information on the study that might be helpful to you.

I stand outside the coffee shop where we agreed to meet, waiting for her. I'm twenty minutes early, not wanting to get lost on the way. Café Daisy is simple on the inside, with wooden tables facing wide-open windows, pastel paintings of suns and moons decorating the walls.

I see Yena before she sees me, walking on the other side of the street with earphones on, the wire disappearing into the crocheted tote bag slung over her shoulder. She's wearing a green sundress, her hair held up with a swirly white claw clip, bangs sweeping over her forehead as she stops at the crosswalk, looking left and right for cars.

She spots me. I lift a hand and wave.

She waves back, and as the crossing signal changes, she runs across the street to meet me.

I'm suddenly hit with the feeling of déjà vu, as if this very thing has happened before. It's so strong it's almost physical, like the déjà vu is pressing its fingers against my head. Strange. I shake it off and the feeling disappears. I hold the café door open for Yena. We walk in.

"Thanks for meeting with me," she says as we sit at a table with our drinks, me with an iced coffee full of milk and sugar, her with a matcha latte. She nods at my drink of choice. "Sweet tooth?"

"Just with coffee. It's the only way I like to drink it," I say. "You're not a coffee snob who's going to judge me for my order, are you? My grandpa always gives me a hard time about it."

I say it lightly, as a joke, but at the mention of Harabeoji, her face softens.

"I'm sorry to hear about his condition," she says. "I

imagine you two are close if you're trying so hard to get him into this study."

I twirl the straw around in my coffee, ice cubes clinking against the glass. "Yeah. I've lived with him my whole life. My parents worked a lot so he was the one who took care of me. I guess we got pretty close." I feel suddenly heavy, thinking about him. "We were together in Canada, but he moved back to Korea after his diagnosis. I'm just here visiting him for the summer."

"Ah," she says. After a pause, she adds, "I'm actually from Canada too."

"No way! Where?"

"Vancouver."

What a small world. "I lived there for a long time before moving to Edmonton," I say. "I wonder if we were ever in the same place at the same time."

"Why?" she says with a curious smile. "Do I look familiar?"

There is something oddly reminiscent about her, like a book I read as a kid that I don't remember the title of. But I don't want to sound weird, so I just laugh and say, "Nah. Vancouver's just small. So, what are you doing here in Busan?"

"My mom is the founder of Sori Clinic. Let's just say she was more than a little distressed that her only daughter had no plans after high school, so she brought me here to work for her until I get my act together."

Her tone is breezy, relaxed and open like she doesn't have a care in the world. But there's something in the way her shoulders tense up and her hands wrap a little tighter around her mug that makes me wonder if she's as chill about it as she sounds. Maybe I shouldn't read so much into it though. I hardly know her.

"Wait. Your mom is Dr. Mira Bae?" I say, their last names suddenly clicking into place for me. "Wow."

"That's right, you're basically talking to memory science royalty," Yena says, her face going serious. She sits up straight, holds out her hand like a princess for me to take. "Charmed."

I laugh but feel my cheeks warm as I take her hand lightly in my own. I wonder if she knows how cute she is. "Well, I'm lucky to receive your help. Thank you."

"About that." She pulls her hand away, leaning back in her seat with an apologetic frown. "I did some digging, but the study is completely full. It'll probably take you six months at the earliest to get off the waitlist."

My stomach sinks. "But I'm leaving at the end of the summer."

"Is there anyone else who would be able to accompany your grandpa into the study when there's space?"

Harabeoji's scathing voice comes back to me. *You don't play around with people's memories.* There's still a chance that I could convince him if I'm here, but if I'm not? There's no way he would do it on his own, and I have no idea if

Samchon would approve of something like this. He's been diligent about getting Harabeoji the support and care he needs in Korea, but that doesn't mean he would be on board for anything more nontraditional.

"I don't think so," I say.

Yena hesitates and then reaches into her tote bag, pulling out a thin, black rectangular device and sliding it across the table.

"What's this?" I ask.

"A recording device that Sori Clinic has its patients use to collect sounds," Yena says. "Do you know how memory erasing works?"

She looks carefully at my face, as if testing me.

"Just from what I've read online," I say. "It's done through sound, right? So you bring in a bunch of sound bites related to the thing you want to forget and Sori Clinic uses it to make a map in your mind of what to erase."

She nods. "Yes, that's the gist of it. So right now, they're trying to see if they can do the opposite: restore memories that have been lost through the same method. Or at least, strengthen weakening memories through sound so those at risk of losing them can hold on to their memories for a little longer. And that begins with this." She taps the recording device with her finger. "I asked around, and the first part of the study is for all participants to bring in sound recordings of the memories they want to remember or strengthen."

I pick up the recording device, turn it over in my hands. "That's step one?"

"That's step one," she says. "I know you're not officially part of the study. But I was thinking, if you want, you can still start doing what all the other participants are doing. And if there's an opening sooner than later, I'll put your name forward and say you're already caught up and ready to go. It's not a guarantee, but it could at least bump you to the top of the waitlist."

A dozen thoughts fly through my mind at once. Even if it's not a guarantee, doing something is better than doing nothing. Being on step one is still a step forward from zero. It's incredibly generous of Yena to offer this to me. I hold her eyes with mine, trying to understand why she's helping me. She shifts uncomfortably under my gaze.

"You don't want to do it?" she says.

"No. I definitely want to. I just don't get why you're doing this for me."

Yena drums her fingers against the table and looks up at the suns and moons on the walls. "My mom thinks I have no future and my supervisor thinks I lack passion. My dad doesn't disagree with them either." She looks back at me, cocking her head to the side. "I think they might be right. I can't think of anything I've really wanted to do in a long time. But for some reason, I want to help you. And there's got to be something to that, right?"

The feeling that there's more to what she's saying than

she's letting on comes back. Her expression is honest but guarded, and I don't know what to say or what to ask or if it's even my business to pry further.

Her hair is falling loose from her claw clip and she tugs it out, retwisting her hair and pinning it back into place. It hits me again, the strong, nearly visceral déjà vu from when she was crossing the street, as if I've seen her do that same motion before. And I can't explain it, but I understand when she says, *For some reason, I want to help you.* Because for some reason, I'm drawn to her too. I don't know what it is, but I feel like a magnet being pulled into her orbit. And even though a part of me is saying that I've already taken up too much of her time and her kindness, another part of me doesn't want this to be the end, is already thinking of a way to see her again.

"Thank you," I say. "I really appreciate it. Would it be too much to bug you for one more favor?"

She raises her eyebrows. "What is it?"

I hold up the recording device. "Go with me to collect a couple sounds? Just until I get the hang of it. I don't want to mess up on step one."

Yena grins and my heart lifts. "Sure. I think I can do that."

SOUND

THE LAWN MOWER
13 YEARS OLD

He was always waiting for her, that boy was. On Saturday mornings when the grass was long and it was time for my morning stroll around the field, he would be standing at the crosswalk, watching for her. Now and then she would be on time but mostly she was late, jumping up and down and waving at him from across the street.

"Wait for the light to change!" he'd cry when she'd throw a quick glance both ways and run across before the signal.

They'd run together, off to wherever they were going. Perhaps some kind of school, by the looks of their backpacks.

Sometimes they'd have umbrellas for rainy days, open against the showers or tucked under their arms in preparation for potential storms. Sometimes he'd be holding a snack for her—a braided, sugary donut, a juice box, a rice ball. And sometimes she'd share her earphones with him as they walked, footsteps perfectly in time with each other.

"That lawn mower is always so loud," she said once, passing him an earbud.

83

"I kind of like it," he said. "Keeps me company when you're always so late."

She stuck her tongue out at him.

The weather changed, the details changed. But one thing stayed the same.

He waited for her and every time she arrived, his face would light up like it was his first time seeing her. By the time she crossed the street to join him, he would try to hide it behind a mask of casual coolness, as if it was just another day.

The truth? It was just another day. It was many of those very simple ordinary days.

But I couldn't help but wonder if that was the reason his eyes lit up so. Because every time he saw her, he was reminded that he got to enjoy his "just another days" with her.

7

YENA

He's the same, but he's different.

I watch his back as he walks ahead of me, leading the way. He was always more serious, thoughtful, putting others before himself. Those things were instantly familiar, and there were other little things about him that made me laugh to myself and think, *Of course*. Of course he'd drink his coffee basically white; as a kid, he would secretly add extra cream and sugar to his grandpa's coffee mug because he couldn't understand why anyone would like it without. Of course he would already be standing outside the café waiting for me; when has he ever not been on time, even when we were kids?

But there are surprises too. He's more tense than I remember, more withdrawn inside his own head. I used to be able to read him like a book, but now I can't tell what he's thinking. Maybe that's just what happens though when you have years and distance and a whole memory-erasing procedure between you. You know. Just a hunch.

"Where are we going?" I ask.

My knowledge of Busan isn't great, but I know we're in an area called Cheongsapo. I recognize the twin red and white lighthouses from a magazine in Sori's waiting room. We walk along the water, where fishing boats are bobbing in the waves. I've always loved the sea and I'm tempted to take a closer look at the colorful boats, but Lucas is already crossing the street, moving quickly away from the water toward a row of cafés and restaurants bustling with people.

"There's a famous sightseeing train around here that I thought I could record," he says. "The Beach Train. Have you been?"

I shake my head. "I haven't explored much of the city. I wouldn't even know where to go, to be honest."

He looks surprised. "Really? My uncle has been texting me nonstop recommendations since I got here. I think he feels bad that he can't take me around himself because of work, but honestly, he's probably given me enough stuff to check out to last me two years."

I laugh, but I can't help but wonder if Mom feels bad for not being able to show me around Busan. She hasn't so much as recommended a single café to me. Wait. Does Dr. Bae even go to cafés? I don't think I've seen her go anywhere outside of home and the clinic.

"I can share his list with you if you want," Lucas says.

"Sure," I say, though my heart isn't fully in it.

We pass the restaurants and cafés and approach the station, where there are already several people waiting with their cameras to capture the incoming train. The tracks run right through the street, and above us, there's a sky rail with colorful capsules slowly moving along it like Easter eggs on a conveyor belt.

"What's that?" I ask, tilting my head up to look at the capsules. There are people sitting inside them as if on an amusement park ride.

"That's the Sky Capsule. I think you can ride it to Hae-undae Beach from here," Lucas says.

"So cute," I say. I didn't know there was something like this in Busan. Maybe I should get that list from Lucas after all.

We stand near the tracks, waiting for the train to pass by. Another thing I wasn't expecting from Lucas: for him to invite me along to collect sounds. After all, to him I'm still a stranger. But he seems focused on doing everything he can to get this process right for his grandfather.

My heart pangs at that. I remember Harabeoji. He was funny, he loved to cook, and he was always kind to me. I saw him around more than I ever saw Lucas's parents. I was never close to my own grandparents growing up, so I secretly felt that Harabeoji was kind of like my grandfather too. I told Lucas that I want to help him, and I do for lots of reasons, some more complicated and maybe even selfish than others. But there's a part of me that also genuinely wants to help Harabeoji too.

"Why the train?" I ask.

At first, I think he's not going to respond. He puts his hands in his pockets and stares down the train tracks. An awkward silence passes and I'm about to tell him that he doesn't have to share if he doesn't want to when he says, "It was the first trip we ever took, just the two of us. We'd just moved to Edmonton and I was having a hard time adjusting."

My palms go clammy. I wipe them on my dress, and ask as casually as I can, "Why'd you move?"

"The housing's more affordable in Alberta," he says. "Also, my family runs a restaurant. It wasn't doing too well in Vancouver and my parents wanted to revive it somewhere new. It was a good choice. We're doing much better now than we were before we moved."

"Ah." There's something thorny and bruised starting to poke at my insides, making my words feel raw when they leave my mouth. "Must've been hard to leave all your friends behind though."

He shrugs. "Not really. I had a few friends that I played sports with at school, but no one I was that close to. Saying goodbye definitely wasn't the hardest part."

I know he doesn't mean for it to hurt the way it does, but his offhand comment cuts straight through me. Now it's my turn to fall silent and stick my hands into my pockets, looking down at my feet. Maybe it was a bad idea, spending time with Lucas. For so long, I've been curious about what he's been up to, but now that I'm actually hearing it, I just feel wrong, like I'm not supposed to be here.

"I think it was the sudden change in environment that was hardest, you know?" he says. "My parents needed my help more than ever to set up the restaurant, and I was so overwhelmed by everything, I started getting nightmares and migraines. My grandpa wanted to take some stress off my shoulders, so he took me on a weekend train trip to the Rocky Mountains for fresh air."

He turns to me with a smile and I'm struck by the sameness of it, the crushing familiarity. "We probably couldn't afford it at all at the time, but man, it was the best weekend ever. We still talk about it. Or we used to. I'm not sure if he'd remember it anymore." At that, his smile fades a bit, and the Lucas that I knew fades back into the Lucas of the present.

"Hence the train," I manage to say, pulling myself out of my own head and gesturing to the tracks before us.

"Hence the train," he agrees. "Some of my best memories are with Harabeoji. If he forgets them and I'm the only one left to remember then it feels almost like, did it even really happen? Or did I imagine the whole thing? It's like sharing a language with someone and then one day waking up to realize you're the only one who speaks it anymore. You still have it, but if no one else does, it's just . . . not the same."

He shakes his head apologetically, cheeks turning pink. "Sorry. I don't know why I shared all that. This probably doesn't make any sense."

Except of course it makes complete sense. Everything he said is exactly how I feel, put into words in a way I haven't been able to express myself. How does he do that, even now? Know me better than I do? Only he doesn't, not really. He doesn't know how much I relate, and he never can.

I want to say it's okay. I want to say I get it. I want to say, what about our language? We had one too. Why did you erase it? Why did you leave me to speak it alone?

"The train's coming!" someone exclaims.

There's a sudden flurry of movement in the people waiting for the train. Lucas quickly fishes the recording device out of his pocket.

"Do I just press record?" he says.

"Yeah," I manage to respond, barely holding it together. "And then just press the same button again when you're done."

He does, holding it up just as the Beach Train approaches. It's white and blue with the words *Haeundae Blueline Park* written across the side. The whole thing has a vintage design, as if someone plucked a toy train from a child's bedroom and made it life-size for passengers to ride along the coast. There's something quaint and nostalgic about it. I can see the appeal and understand why there are so many people not just riding the train but standing around to take photos.

The train whistle blows as it pulls into the station. I watch the blue of it pass us by, and I hear my own voice echo in my head.

Meet me at blue hour.

Lucas turns to me and smiles, pressing the button to stop the recording. "Do you want to ride the Sky Capsule? My treat for helping me out with all of this."

"Actually, I have to go now," I say. My voice comes out tight with the threat of oncoming tears. This is too much. Why did I see him today? Why did I think it would be fine?

His smile falters as he senses my change in mood. "Is everything okay?"

"Uh-huh. Totally fine. You've got the hang of the recording device now, right?"

"I think so . . ." His brow furrows, as if he's trying to figure out what happened. But I'm already walking away, both hands gripped tight around my bag for something to hold on to, because if I stay one more minute, I know I'll completely fall apart.

And how could I even begin to explain that?

I end up at Haeundae Beach.

Lucas always hated crowds, but there's something about them that I find comforting. Like I'm part of something bigger than myself. Here, in the mob of people fighting for a spot to lay their towels and pitch their umbrellas, it doesn't matter that I'm lost and directionless and completely torn up inside. No one is watching me. I'm just another anonymous face.

I take my shoes off and sit down in the sand, stretching

my legs in front of me and pulling out my Walkman. I stick in my earphones, finger hovering over the play button. I haven't stopped thinking about Lucas's tape since I first heard it, but at the same time, I haven't been able to bring myself to listen to it again. I do now, hitting play before I can overthink it, closing my eyes to the static.

The wind chimes start. The film reel, the water. I try to guess which memories link up to which sounds. Some are easier to recognize than others, but I do my best to pay attention to all of them, the last remaining pieces of evidence that our language was once shared.

I brace myself for the sound of the ice cream truck, but when it comes, it still makes my toes curl. I don't have to guess which memory this one's supposed to be. Unlike some of the others, which could span across many different moments, this one is painfully specific. The day is as vivid as ever: fourteen years old, ice cream melting in our hands, sitting on the curb by the truck. We were the only customers. I remember turning to him to say something funny but by coincidence, he turned to face me at the exact same time. I remember our noses were too close and the sunlight made his eyes a lighter brown and my heart was doing funny things that it only ever did around him.

Up until that point, I'd imagined a hundred different ways that I would tell him how I felt, that maybe I saw him as more than a best friend. But in all my imaginings, I didn't think I'd blurt out "I think I love you" on a random day, on a random street, sitting inches from his face with ice cream dripping down my fist. After that, it's a bit of a blur. I think he looked surprised, and I think there was a group of kids who came running to the truck so we had to get up from our spot. I know I got flustered and ran home before he could reply.

In hindsight, maybe I should have stayed, because that was the last time I ever saw him. Right afterward, he disappeared from my life.

That is, until now. Was my confession so awful that he decided to erase me from his mind? Ugh. Thinking about it makes me want to bury myself on the beach and die.

The tape ends and I pull out my earphones, balling them in my fist. "I am the most embarrassing person in the world!" I wail to the sky. I don't even care that people on the beach turn to look at me. Let them stare. The truth is the truth.

"Now why would you think that?" a voice behind me says.

I turn, startled. Joanne and Tony from Sori Clinic are standing there, staring at me. A bag of convenience store snacks dangles from Joanne's arm and Tony is holding a case of energy drinks.

Well, this is awkward. Nothing like your coworkers walking in during the middle of your mental breakdown. I try to think of a cover story, but my mind goes blank. "What are you two doing here?" I say instead. Very good,

Yena, excellent diversion tactic.

"It's going to be a late night at the office so we're getting sustenance for everyone," Joanne says. "Or at least, I was. Tony insisted on giving me a hand."

"Isn't there a store right by the office?" I ask. "What are you doing all the way at the beach?"

"Tony also insisted on taking the long way back."

"I just had to get out of the office for a bit," Tony groans, dropping the case of energy drinks next to me and sitting down. "Don't tell your mom, but she's driving me up the wall."

"Dr. Bae is?" I say in surprise.

Joanne sighs, sitting down on the other side of me. She rummages around in her bag of snacks and passes me a bag of Honey Butter Chips. "Your mom is under a lot of pressure for the recovery study to go well and it hasn't been going as smoothly as she'd hoped. She's stressed and it's been affecting the rest of the staff."

"It's been going as smoothly as anyone should expect it to be at this stage," Tony says, massaging his temples. "It hasn't even been a week yet! She has unrealistic expectations and she's pushing us all too hard. And I say this as someone who considers himself her number one professional fan."

I open the bag of chips, popping one into my mouth. "Does that mean you're a full-time fan or you're a fan who's professional about being one?"

"The latter," he says, snapping his fingers and pointing

at me. "There is literally nobody else in the field of memory science that's doing the things that Dr. Bae does. I studied her career throughout my whole time in grad school. It was a dream come true landing a job with her after graduation. I respect the hell out of her. But she is an overworking demon boss."

I burst out laughing at that, a chip nearly flying out of my mouth.

"Tony," Joanne says in a warning voice. "Yena's her daughter."

"So she probably knows exactly what I'm talking about," Tony says. "Don't you, Yena?"

I nod. I might not know in as much detail as they do, but of course I know that she's a workaholic with impossibly high standards. That's just who she is, how she's always been. People I meet usually rave about this side of her, but it's refreshing to hear someone talk so candidly about the other side of the coin.

"Well, you know. Dr. Bae works twice as hard because there are twice as many people out there who are looking for any opportunity to discredit her. It's not easy being a woman in such a controversial field," Joanne says. She pauses. "Though I would love to take a vacation sometime."

"I agree with all of the above," Tony says. "She's amazing. And so are vacations."

They both sigh deeply and the three of us sit in silence for a moment, staring at the ocean waves. I think about what Joanne just said, how memory erasing is a controversial field. I know it is in theory but honestly, I've never thought too deeply about it. I figured that those who want to do it can, and those who are anti-erasure can simply stay away from it.

But after everything with Lucas, I can't help but wish that erasure didn't exist at all. I never thought about how painful it would be for those on the other side. The erased side.

"Do you think erasure is a good thing?" I ask out loud.

"Ah, my family's favorite holiday dinner topic," Tony says dryly. "Splendid."

"I'm being genuine!"

"I am too. My honest answer? It's not a good thing. And it's not a bad thing. It's technology that now exists in our world that you can choose to use how you'd like, much like many other things. But beyond good and bad, memory erasing is inevitable. As soon as it was discovered, there was no going back. We'll never live in a world without it again, but it's still in its early stages. There are still a lot of unknowns around *how* it will exist in our society, and I want to be part of that conversation."

I nod, following along. I've never thought about it like that before, but I suppose it makes sense. "Is that what you tell your family at holidays?"

"Yes, I'm very popular at parties."

"My sister did the erasure procedure," Joanne says

thoughtfully. "She wanted to erase certain memories of our father after he passed away. He was a complicated and abusive person, and she said she would rather live with the consequences of erasure than continue carrying the burden of past things that will never be resolved. I didn't make the same choice as her, but knowing everything I do about her and our father, I can understand why she did it."

I sit with the weight of that, turning it over in my head. They were both so honest and forthcoming with me that I find myself saying, "I met my childhood best friend again the other day and found out he erased me."

Joanne squeezes my arm. "That must have been a tough discovery."

"Yeah," I say, voice cracking. "I want to talk to my mom about it, but you know. She's been busy."

It's mostly true. I did have a moment alone with her in the staff room yesterday, and we did cross paths at home earlier this morning. But the timing wasn't ideal. When she asked how my day was going, I said, "All good," thinking, *She's in a rush. I can't get into it now.* At least, that's what I keep telling myself as I try to ignore the growing pit in my stomach.

I want to talk to her, but I don't. I want answers, but I don't. It's like how I feel around Lucas: I want all the details about the past four years of his life, but actually hearing them is too much. What if I don't like what I find out? Scratch that. I'm almost positive I *won't* like what I find out, if recent events have been any indication. How can I be so desperate to know the truth but so scared of it at the same time?

When you know, you can't unknow, and I'm terrified of how I'll feel when I can't ignore it anymore, of how it might consume me whole.

"I'll convince her to take a break," Tony says. "God knows we all need one."

"Speaking of breaks, we should probably get these back to the staff so they can have one," Joanne says, gesturing to her snack bag.

They both give me an encouraging pat on the shoulder before standing and wiping the sand off their clothes. I wasn't expecting to find solace today, especially in them, but despite everything I feel a lot better than when I first arrived at the beach. "Thanks, you two," I say. "For the talk."

"No problem," Joanne says. "You should join us for our next team dinner. It'd be great to have you, but no pressure of course."

I didn't think I would ever consider going to a team dinner or getting to know my coworkers during my summer here, but maybe it's not such a bad idea. "Okay. I'll think about it," I say, meaning it.

"Oh, and Yena?" Tony says, picking up the case of energy drinks.

"Yeah?"

"If you do see that friend of yours again, you'll want to be careful. If he had you entirely erased from his memories, that means it was a pretty big procedure and he might be more prone to side effects if he's exposed to too many triggers."

I frown, worried. "What kind of side effects?"

"Migraines, nausea, hallucinations, confusion . . . there's a wide range. It's typically quite minimal, but erasing a few memories is one thing. Wiping out a whole person's existence can be significantly more sensitive. Just something to keep in mind."

They wave goodbye as they head back to the office. I wave too, mulling over what Tony said as I put my shoes back on and start to gather my things. My phone lights up in my bag and I realize I missed a string of messages from Lucas.

Lucas:

Hey, just wanted to see if you're okay. You seemed troubled when you left.

Lucas:

Thinking about going to record some sounds at the fish market this week if you want to come with?

Lucas:

Since you said you haven't explored much of the city yet . . . thought it might be fun to have someone to go through my uncle's list with haha.

My fingers hover over the screen. After the emotional disaster that was today, I shouldn't see him again. Especially not if I might trigger side effects for him. That would be bad. Really bad.

But for some reason, I can't seem to bring myself to say no. If I let him go now, I'll probably never see him again. And then what? Do I just go on living like I was? Stuck and never knowing why he did what he did?

I let my impulses take over. I type, hit send, stuff my phone back in my bag before I can take it back.

Me:

Count me in.

8

LUCAS

Samchon said Jagalchi Market is the biggest seafood market in Korea and he wasn't kidding. Yena and I meet at the main building and as soon as we step inside, we're surrounded by rows and rows of booths selling abalone, squid, clams, octopus, and the biggest shrimp I've ever seen in my life. And that's not even the half of it. I've gone shopping for restaurant ingredients with Harabeoji before, but I've never been anywhere quite like this. It's wet, it's bustling, and it definitely smells like fish guts.

Older women in colorful aprons and rubber gloves run the stalls, ushering us over to take a look at their offerings. I wonder if Yena is as overstimulated by everything as I am, but her eyes are huge with delight and she's already running ahead to look at the fish.

Honestly, I'm a little surprised she agreed to meet me today. I wasn't sure how things would be between us after she left so abruptly the last time I saw her. But when we met outside the market, she apologized before I could even bring it up, saying she had to go in a rush because she wasn't feeling well. I can't help but think there's more to it than that, but as much as I want to ask what really happened, she seems so happy now that I don't push it.

"Everything is so fresh!" Yena exclaims.

Fresh is an understatement. The fish in the tanks are still alive, splashing and swimming around in the water. I spot a crab trying to crawl its way out of its tank.

"I'll give it to you at a good price," the woman at the stall says in Korean, poking the crab back into place. "You can take it up to the second floor to eat right away."

"Ahh." Yena nods in understanding, replying in Korean. "We'll look around the whole place first."

I realize I've only ever heard Yena speak English, which makes sense because that's what we're comfortable with. But it's funny how your voice can change with the language you speak and how it can bring out a different side of you.

"What?" Yena says, and I realize that I'm staring at her.

My cheeks warm and I quickly look up to the bright ceiling lights. "Nothing."

"Judging my Korean?" she guesses. She must see the surprise on my face because she gives me a teasing grin. "I know, I'm awful. I was the worst student in Korean school."

"I was thinking about your Korean, but not that you're awful," I say. "Just that it makes you sound different."

"Oh yeah?" She starts moving again, walking backward to look at me. She tilts her head to the side. "Different how?"

"Different like . . . more uncertain? But not in a bad

way." I think it over. "More like in a curious and open way. Your voice is gentler."

"Hm. I should try to speak Korean more often," she says. "I can't think of the last time someone's called me curious and gentle. I kind of like that."

"I like how you sound in any language," I say.

Her eyes widen. Whoa. Who said that? I'm not usually the type to be so forward with anyone about anything, let alone a girl I met less than a week ago. But there's something about Yena that makes my words have a mind of their own. Even when we were waiting for the Beach Train, I realized she was the first person I've confided in about Harabeoji and why protecting his memories is so important to me.

Maybe it's the nonjudgmental vibe about her that makes me so comfortable.

Maybe it's the fact that she *is* basically a stranger and it doesn't feel as hard to tell her the truth.

Or maybe there's something between us, a reason I've been drawn to her from the moment she ran into me on the street. I've never believed in love at first sight or experienced anything close to it, but could this be that? Or something like it? Something like an instant connection and ease?

Yena is still walking backward and she's about to collide right into a tank of live eels. I quickly reach out and grab her arm, pulling her away just in time. She stumbles against me, palm pressed against my chest. For a moment, she doesn't move and I wonder if she can feel my heart beating faster.

I think I'm holding my breath. I think she might be too.

And then she takes a step back, dropping her hand, and says, "Sannakji!"

I blink. "What?"

"I just remembered. I was looking up Jagalchi Market yesterday and reading recommendations on what to eat, and one of the things on the list was sannakji. There's octopus somewhere around here, right?"

She hurries forward. I let out a breath and follow.

"Have you had it before?" Yena asks, stopping in front of a booth featuring a tank of small octopuses. "Sannakji?"

"Um. No. That's live octopus, isn't it?" I've seen videos of people eating it, the tentacles still moving and crawling up their chopsticks as they popped it into their mouths. "My parents told me it's a choking hazard."

"Come on. I read the octopus isn't actually alive. It's just the nerves that are still active. It'll be fun. And delicious."

I shake my head. "You can help yourself."

"Oh, I will." She waves at the woman working the stall. "Ajumma! One small octopus, please."

Somehow, moments later, I find myself sitting across from Yena at a table on the second-floor food court, a plate of wriggling octopus pieces between us. "It's actually moving," I say, unable to look away.

"That's the best part," Yena says cheerfully. "Jal meok-getseumnida!"

She claps her hands together and then picks up a piece

with her chopsticks, dipping it in some sesame sauce before putting it into her mouth. I stare at her from across the table as she chews, her eyes slowly widening. She covers her mouth with her hand and says, "I think it's suctioned to my cheek."

"Oh my god," I say.

She swallows and laughs. "But it actually tastes so good! Are you sure you don't want to try? You love seafood."

I raise my eyebrows. I do love seafood, but I don't think I've ever mentioned that to her. "How did you know that?"

"Oh. Just a guess. You seem like you'd like it." She clears her throat and picks up another big piece of octopus, sticking it into her mouth.

"Careful. You have to chew it a lot so it doesn't get stuck," I warn.

Before she can respond, she starts coughing, mildly at first and then harder.

"Yena?" I say.

She shakes her head, unable to speak, pointing at her mouth and pounding at her chest.

"Holy shit, you're actually choking." Panic overtakes me and I leap to my feet, rushing to her side. I'm about to start hitting her back when she lets out a big cough, spitting her food out into a napkin. She inhales deeply, tears in her eyes.

"Whew, that was close," she laughs, taking a sip of water.

"Are you okay?" I ask, worried.

"Totally fine. Noted on chewing more."

I sigh, sitting back down, my panic ebbing into a mix of relief and annoyance. "I told you to be careful. You are so reckless."

"So I hear," she says dryly, chewing carefully on another piece. "You know, this is good, but it's too much food for me. I don't think I'll finish it."

"What? That's such a waste," I say. Harabeoji raised me to never leave leftovers unless I'm planning on eating them the next day. "You can't take this home."

She shrugs. "I'll just leave it here."

I press my lips together and then, after a beat, I sigh and pick up my chopsticks. "Fine. I'll help you."

"I didn't ask you to," she says in a singsong voice, and I know she knows exactly what she's doing. How did she know that leftovers are my weakness?

Gingerly, I pick up a piece of octopus and dip it into the spicy sauce. It squirms around in my chopsticks. It's fine. It's normal. It's not really alive. That's what I tell myself to get over the mental hurdle of eating something that's still moving like it's trying to get away. I hesitate just for a second and then I put it into my mouth, chewing furiously and swallowing.

"Well?" Yena says.

"It's . . . good. Really good, actually. I like it."

"Ha! I knew you would," she says, looking pleased. "I mean because it tastes good, so of course you would," she adds.

I had a plan for today. Come to Jagalchi Market, record a few sounds for Harabeoji's memories, and get to know Yena more. Nowhere on my Notes app did I have anything about eating sannakji and liking it, but here we are. We polish off the whole plate and all the sauces that came with it.

Afterward, I pull out the recording device and capture some sounds around the market: dishes clattering around the food court, voices speaking in Korean as deals are made between vendors and customers. These are the things that remind me of Harabeoji, that make me think of the meals we've shared, the deals I've watched him make. By the time we leave, I do end up checking off everything on my plan. It feels good.

Being outside also feels good, as hot as it is today. We sit on a bench by the water where people are taking photos next to a giant I HEART JAGALCHI sign. Yena points to my recording device and asks, "Did you get what you needed?"

"I think so," I say. "I just hope I get to use it in the study."

"I hope a spot opens for you soon too," she says.

"It's not just that. Once a spot does open up, I have to convince my grandpa to actually take it. He's not that keen on memory tampering."

"Oh?" Yena looks out at the water, putting her feet up on the bench and tucking her knees into her chest. "Why's that?"

"He says it's unnatural and that memories aren't something to be played around with."

She silently twists her hair around her fingers, looping it up and securing it in place with a claw clip. "Maybe he's right," she says after a moment.

I look at her in surprise. I guess I just assumed that Yena was pro–memory tampering, considering the fact that she works at Sori Clinic and her mom is the founder. Not to mention she's been helping me prepare for the recovery study this whole time. "What do you mean?"

"I mean maybe it is unnatural and shouldn't be played around with." There's a hardness in Yena's face now that I'm not sure how to read. I feel suddenly defensive. If this is what she believes, then what does she really think about my plan? Does she think that what I'm doing is wrong?

"I don't agree," I say. "I think it's a great opportunity."

"Okay, sure. Maybe for recovery, but what about erasure? Do you think all memory tampering is a great opportunity?"

She turns to look at me now, a challenge in her eyes. I don't get it. What does this have to do with erasure? What is she even trying to challenge me about?

I shrug. "Yeah, for some people, I think it would be great. Depending on their circumstances."

Her jaw tightens. "Well, I hope things are working out awesome for those people. But messing with memories isn't for everyone. Maybe you should consider listening to your grandpa when he tells you that."

"He'll come around," I say, the defensive feeling growing sharper. "He just doesn't know what's best for him yet." Hearing how it sounds out loud makes me wince inside, but I don't take it back.

"And you do?" she says.

"Yes."

"How do you know?"

"Because I know."

"How?"

"Because I have a plan!"

I don't mean to raise my voice, but I can't help it. Her questions are getting under my skin and I can feel my frustration rising.

"Why are you even helping me if you don't believe in what I'm doing?" I snap. The words come out harsher than I want them to.

She blinks and then looks away again, dropping her feet to the ground. "Good question. Maybe I won't do that anymore."

How did we get here? A few minutes ago, we were having a great day. And now we're fighting about . . . what exactly? I don't even know. I sigh, trying to swallow my anger and pride.

"Listen, can we just take a step back? What's going on?" I say. Or at least, I start to say it. I barely get the first word out when a sharp, piercing pain shoots across my skull.

I wince, hand flying up to the side of my head. Yena

turns back to look at me, the hardness in her face instantly changing to concern.

"Lucas? Are you okay?" she asks, putting a hand on my shoulder. "What's going on?"

"I don't know, I just got this sudden headache," I say. My vision goes a bit white around the edges and I blink a few times, trying to clear it. It gets better, but my head feels like it's splitting open. "It might be a migraine. I used to get them a lot a few years ago, but it's been a while. And it's never been this bad before."

Yena chews on her lower lip, worried. "We should get you home. Come on. I'll call a taxi."

"Yena?" I want to tell her that I'm not sure what happened between us just now and that I'm sorry for snapping at her. But the pain is making it hard to think straight and Yena is already on her feet, waving down a cab. Even after we climb into the back seat and she rides in the taxi with me to make sure I get home safe, I can't form the words. "Thank you" is all I can manage.

"Get some rest," she says, and then I'm home and she's gone and I can't help but think that even though many things went according to plan today, there were many more things that truly did not.

SOUND

THE WIND CHIME
13 YEARS OLD AND JUST 13 YEARS OLD

The boy's grandfather helped him make me with glass beads and seashells. I could tell by how careful he was in putting me together that he wanted me to look good and to sing well. I felt like I could make him proud. Sometimes talent just knows.

"What are you doing?" his father asked.

"Making a wind chime for Yena's birthday."

He didn't see the look his father gave his mother behind his back. His grandfather saw it though and said, "Why? Don't you think it's a wonderful gift?"

"Do you think you're maybe spending too much time with Yena these days?" his mother asked. "What about your other friends?"

"I hang out with them all the time at school," the boy said, concentrating on the shells. "I only get to see Yena on weekends."

His father shakes his head. "You're always late to Korean school because you wait for her. I don't like how you've made it a habit."

"You know, the weekend could be time you spend at the restaurant instead," his mother said. "Now that you're older, you've become a real help. We love having you there."

She ruffled the boy's hair affectionately. The boy pressed his lips together and looked to his grandfather for help.

"Yena's a great friend. Let him make her a great gift," his grandfather said. "And I think Lucas spends plenty of time at the restaurant as it is."

"All right, all right," his mother said.

Soon I was complete. I was dazzling in the light. It was time for my first performance.

The boy placed me carefully in a bag with tissue paper and got on his bike, riding to the girl's apartment. When she opened the door, he thrust the bag into her hands, too nervous to wait.

"Happy birthday," he said.

"Wow! Thanks. Come in."

We went inside, where her father greeted him, saying, "Lucas! You're just in time for cake."

She opened the bag and pulled me out, gasping. "Did you make this?"

"Yeah," he said, shy. He cleared his throat. "Harabeoji helped me."

"Dad, look! Lucas made me a wind chime. How did you know I always wanted one? Wait, is this because of that one time we went into that store and I wanted to get the wind chime hanging there but it wasn't for sale?"

"Did you say that? I don't remember."

Liar. He told that exact story to his grandfather while they were putting me together.

"It's beautiful, Lucas," the girl's father said. "Where should I hang it up?"

The girl picked a spot by the window but insisted on hanging me up herself, nearly falling off a chair in the process. I went up and this was it. My moment. She pushed the window open, letting the breeze in.

And for the first time ever, I sang.

"It's perfect," she said.

"Yeah," the boy replied, looking at her.

"Who wants ice cream cake?" her father said.

That day, I gave encore after encore, and I found what I was meant to do. It was only the first of many performances, but it was the one that began it all. I made the boy proud, and I was just as the girl said. Perfect.

9

YENA

"So let me get this straight. You met the so-called friend that erased you because he's in Busan trying to get his grandpa into the recovery study. You told him that you'll help him get into said study. And then you spent a bunch of time with him helping him record sounds?"

"Um. What's your definition of a bunch of time? Because it was really only two days."

Danielle stares at me from across the table. "You're a bit sadistic, aren't you?"

It's a couple of days after my hangout with Lucas and I'm back at work. Danielle and I are taking a lunch break in the staff room, a small space at the back of the clinic with a microwave, an electric kettle, a table for two spread with our take-out burgers, and I just finished filling her in on everything that's happened since I last saw her.

Dad still hasn't gotten back to me, a fact that's been bothering me more and more with each passing day. How much effort does it take to reply to one measly text message? An SOS message at that? Whatever. That's just the way Dad is. I should be used to it by now.

I haven't talked to Mom yet either. I almost brought it up the other day when we were at home at the same time. She was making instant coffee and I got so far as to say, "Hey, Mom?"

"Yeah?" she said.

The words raced through my mind in the span of a second. *Did you know Lucas erased me? Do you know why he did it? How could you keep this from me? How could you how could you how could you?* "Could you . . . make me a coffee too?" I asked instead.

I've put off talking to her for this long. What's a little longer?

So in a strange turn of events, Danielle has become the only one who has any idea what's going on in my life right now in more detail. I mean, I'll take it. I need *someone* to debrief with.

"I wouldn't say sadistic," I say, picking at my french fries. "Curious feels more accurate. Wouldn't you be if you were me?"

"If I were you, Lucas would be dead to me," Danielle says flatly. "Aren't you mad at him for what he did?"

"Yes. No. I don't know! I'm not sure if mad is the right word." It's complicated. There's anger in there for sure, but also embarrassment, hurt, confusion, and somewhere in the midst of all that, the thrill of being together again. I can't help it. Despite everything, it feels good to be with him. He's different, I'm different, but there's still something familiar between us, an undeniable connection even after all this time, and it's just so nice to have that back. At least, it was until I ruined everything by getting mad at him and giving him a migraine at the market. We haven't spoken since.

Maybe Danielle's right. Maybe I am sadistic. "How am I supposed to know how to feel when I don't know why he did it?" I say.

"What is there to know? He did what he did." Danielle takes a bite of her burger, looking irritated. "Some things are unforgivable, no matter the reason."

I think back to the day Danielle helped me find Lucas's file on the laptop. What did she say to me again? *I know how shitty it is to be forgotten.* There's obviously more going on here, but I'm not sure how to ask.

"Who hurt you?" I say, going for the lighthearted approach. She shoots me a look. Ack. Wrong tactic.

"I mean, thank you for being so empathetic and Team Yena about this whole thing," I say humbly. "But I'm just wondering . . . is everything okay with you? This seems personal."

At first, I think she's going to ignore me. But then she lets out a sigh and says, "Do you know how I first heard about Sori Clinic?"

I lean forward, intrigued. Even after weeks of working with Danielle, I hardly know anything about her personal life. "How?" I ask.

"When I was in high school, my mom got sick and passed away. My dad couldn't handle the grief, so you know what he did? He found out about Sori Clinic, flew to Korea, and had her erased from his memory. He thought it would be better to forget her than to live with the pain of missing her."

She says the whole story without looking away from me once. Her voice is flat, almost emotionless, but I can hear the strain in her words.

"Danielle," I say, stricken.

"He may not have erased me and my siblings from his memory, but he left us to deal with our mom's loss by ourselves," she says. "In that way, he forgot about us too. He abandoned us right when we needed him most, and to me, there's no excuse for that kind of thing."

"That totally makes sense," I say quietly. More and more, I'm realizing how far the ripple effects go when someone gets an erasure. I think of all the mixtapes in the Memotery, all the ones I've listened to, all the ones I haven't yet. I only ever thought about the person the tape belonged to, but what about their families? Their friends? Their lovers? All the people who still remember? Where did the erasure leave them?

"Thanks for sharing with me," I say. "I'm really sorry you went through that. And you're right. It is really shitty to be forgotten."

There's a flash of emotion in her eyes and she gives me

a curt nod. She stands, gathering her garbage. "Shall we get back to work?"

"Yeah." I push my chair back, standing too. "Honestly, Danielle, I'm surprised you'd want to work at Sori Clinic after experiencing all of that. Is it tough for you, being here and being reminded of it?"

She shrugs. "It was an opportunity I couldn't refuse. After all, memory erasure is such a specialized and unique field. My college mentor said it could be a great experience for me and my writing. And it's true. There's a lot I can learn here."

Ever the professional. I look at Danielle in a new light. I suppose I always respected her, begrudgingly, but now there's a whole other layer to it. I imagine the level of emotion, of depth, that must appear in her writing with how dedicated she is.

She tosses her burger wrapper into the trash can and shoots me a grin. "Or maybe I'm sadistic, just like you."

I stay longer at the clinic than I need to, long after Danielle clocks out from her shift and my arms start aching from organizing tapes all day. Mostly, I don't want to go home to be alone with my thoughts. At least here, I have something to keep me busy. I shift between shelving tapes and listening to them, but there's only so long you can keep yourself preoccupied with other people's memories. Eventually, I pack up and head out.

"Late night, Yena?" Joanne says as I pass through the lobby. I guess she and Tony have been unsuccessful in their attempt at getting Dr. Bae to slow down. They're looking more and more tired every time I see them around the office, and I can tell that the shadows under Joanne's eyes are getting darker. Regardless of how tired she is though, she gives me a warm smile, holding out a bowl of plum candy that she keeps at her desk.

"Not as late as you, it seems," I say, taking a piece. Joanne always has the best snacks.

"I'll be out of here soon myself. My sister and I have dinner plans tonight."

I pause in the middle of unwrapping the candy. "Hey, can I ask you something personal? You don't have to answer if you don't want to." It's not something I would usually do, striking up a conversation like this out of nowhere, but my earlier talk with Danielle has me in some kind of mood.

"Sure. What's going on?"

"When your sister erased those memories of your dad . . . I know you said you understood her decision, but do you ever wish she didn't do it? Is it hard for you at all, remembering things she doesn't anymore?"

Joanne's face grows thoughtful. "There are hard things, for sure. Avoiding certain topics when it comes to Dad, or not knowing how she'll react when something reminds her of him but she doesn't know why. She erased the parts of him that hurt her the most, but forgetting didn't make that pain go away per se, so it can be hard to see her carry that without being able to talk about why. And you know, there's a certain loneliness that comes with being the only one who remembers something."

I nod emphatically and she smiles at me in understanding. "But at the same time, even without erasure, that's the human experience," she says. "Things you'll remember forever, other people will forget or choose to bury because everyone navigates their emotions in different ways. Even if she hadn't done the procedure, there would have been hard and lonely things."

I consider that. Would there have been hard and lonely things between me and Lucas even if he hadn't erased me? Maybe, yes. I'm sure there would have been, though right now it's hard to imagine anything harder than this. Still, I tuck away Joanne's words in the back of my mind to keep mulling over later.

"Thanks, Joanne. I appreciate it," I say. "Have a good dinner with your sister."

"You have a good night too, Yena. Oh, and stay safe out there. The reporters are back."

"Really? Why?"

I'm surprised. The crowds have pretty much dissipated since the initial launch of the recovery study. I haven't seen anything unusual since.

Joanne hesitates. She beckons me closer, lowering her voice. "I probably shouldn't be telling you this, but I think it's good for all the staff to know, for your own safety. We had a rough day with the study recently. One of the memories they were trying to restore for a patient ended up erasing a closely related memory instead."

I suck in a breath. "You're kidding. So instead of recovering . . . ?"

"They just did more erasing." Joanne says grimly. "Dr. Bae has been keeping it pretty quiet, but I think word leaked out somehow earlier today. We have protestors standing outside now to bring the study to an immediate halt."

Oh man. This is bad news. "How could this happen?"

"I mean, it is still a study, after all. The participants were aware that something like this could happen, and they signed agreements recognizing that. Luckily, it wasn't a sizable memory, but it is unfortunate." She sighs. "Anyway, I just wanted to give you a heads-up. Be careful, okay?"

"Okay. Thanks, Joanne."

I pull out my phone as I wait for the elevator and type a text to Mom.

Me:

> Heard about the study. Are you okay?

My finger hovers over the send button. Would she be upset if she knew that I knew? Would she even want to talk about this with me?

I press backspace, erasing the message. This seems like a conversation that's better suited to being in person.

If I can ever gather the courage to talk to her at all, that is.

I take the elevator down, bracing myself for the people outside. There are a handful of reporters on the street, microphones and cameras pointed toward a bigger group of people, holding protest signs.

SORI CLINIC DOES MORE HARM THAN GOOD.

END MEMORY TAMPERING.

STOP TRYING TO PLAY GOD, DR. BAE.

It's a lot, but I was expecting this thanks to Joanne's warning. I duck my head and try to slip past them.

What I wasn't expecting was for a reporter to look right at me and say, "Bae Yena?"

I make the mistake of looking up.

Immediately, all the microphones and cameras and protestors turn in my direction. The reporters rush forward, closing in around me. I stagger back in shock, but there's nowhere for me to go. I'm surrounded.

"Yena, can you comment on your mom's desire to control other people's memories? What do you think about her mission?"

"Is it true that the study to recover memories has gone haywire? Are the memories of participants being erased against their will?"

"Do you believe that memory tampering is ethical?"

"I—I—" I don't know what to say. I don't know where to go. I don't even know what's going on right now. I'm barely processing these questions, thrown at me in a mix of fast Korean and English, blurring together. How do they know who I am? How do I get out of here?

Just as I feel like I'm about to suffocate under their pressure, I feel a warm hand close softly around mine. I look to the side and see Lucas staring back at me, just on the outside of the circle of reporters. I blink. Am I dreaming? Is that really him? I'm reminded of the first day I ran into him outside the clinic, how I thought I was seeing ghosts. But that's really his hand giving mine a gentle tug and his familiar face that mouths, "Run."

And before I can think too much about it, he pulls me out of the circle of reporters, and I do. I run.

We race down the sidewalk, through a back street, bumping shoulders with everyone we pass, leaving a trail of "I'm sorry!" behind us. At first, I hear footsteps following in our direction, but the farther we go, the quieter they get. Lucas leads me into an alleyway lined with pojangmacha, outdoor restaurants pitched under tents, serving Korean street food and drinks. We duck into one of the tents, grab a corner table away from the entrance. By the time we've put in our order for odeng, I'm certain we've lost them, but my heart is still beating fast. From running, from adrenaline, from *him*.

I look at Lucas across the table and realize I'm still clinging on to his hand. I open my mouth to say something—*Thank you? I'm sorry?*—but the words get drowned out in my mind by the sound of my own racing pulse. His thumb is resting lightly against my wrist and I wonder if he can hear it too, if he can feel it.

The odeng arrives and I reluctantly let go of his hand to make room. The space between my fingers feels colder now and I grab a skewer of fish cakes from the steaming broth in front of me to distract myself.

"Um, thank you," I say, clearing my throat. "For getting me out of that."

"Yeah, of course. Are you okay?" he asks. His cheeks are still red from running, his eyebrows furrowed in concern.

"I'm okay. I think." I lower the skewer without taking a bite and let out a shaky laugh. "That was really overwhelming and unexpected."

"It looked like it," he says. "What happened?"

I hesitate. I'm not sure if I should tell Lucas why the protestors were there. Joanne did share the reason with me in confidence, though if it's already been leaked, it's probably only a matter of time until he hears about it too. "There was a mistake in the recovery study," I admit. "A participant accidentally had one of their memories erased while they were trying to restore a related memory."

"Oh." Lucas frowns, looking lost in serious thought. I wonder if this will change his mind about the study. But he must not want to talk about it because he moves on quickly, saying, "I'm glad I was there to help you out."

I feel secretly relieved. I don't know if I'm ready to talk about erasure with Lucas again. "Yeah, me too. You really saved me. Wait, why *were* you there?"

"Oh. Me?" His cheeks grow even redder and now it's his turn to grab a skewer but not eat it, twirling it around absentmindedly between his fingers as he searches for the words. "To be honest, I've been wanting to text you. Or call you. But I wasn't sure what to say. Things ended kind of weird between us last time we saw each other, and I wanted to say I'm sorry. I feel like I got way too defensive and short with you."

I shake my head. "No, I'm the one who's sorry. I had a lot on my mind that day and I was taking it out on you."

I've thought about our argument outside Jagalchi Market over and over again since it happened, going back and forth between feeling painfully stung by and angry about what he said and regretting that I lost my cool. He doesn't know what I know. I can't expect him to understand why I'm so hurt by some of the things he says. But it's not fair. He *should* know. I didn't choose this. And then the cycle begins again.

I really am sorry though, and this is the closest to the

truth I can tell him right now.

"We're both sorry," he says. "So . . . can we hang out again?"

"What about your migraine?" I ask. Tony warned me that there might be side effects if I spend too much time with Lucas and look what happened. Between all my complicated feelings, there's definitely a strong undercurrent of guilt. "Are you feeling better?"

"Completely better. I slept and when I woke up, it's like it never happened. I haven't collected any sounds since the market though, and it would be great to do that together again."

That's a relief. Still, maybe I should be more cautious. For both his physical condition and my emotional one.

If I were you, Lucas would be dead to me. Danielle's voice rings in my ears.

But Danielle's not me. I'm me. And for better or for worse, I know I can't turn away from Lucas when he's sitting right in front of me like this, waiting for my reply with a hopeful expression on his face. Because when I look at him, it's not just Lucas I see. It's the version of myself that disappeared when he did. Someone who connects with other people and likes new experiences and laughs for real. Seeing Lucas again this summer, I realize that as much as I've missed him, I've missed myself even more.

I still have so many questions: why he left, why he erased me. I don't think I can let him go until I know or find some semblance of peace with that. But there's a part of me that also wants to keep seeing him because maybe if I do, I can bring that lost part of me home again.

The guilt that I might trigger more side effects for him resurfaces. I push it down. He's feeling better now. It'll be fine and I'll keep an eye on him to make sure it stays that way.

"Okay," I say. "Let's go collect some sounds."

10

LUCAS

We find ourselves on Bosu Book Street, an alleyway full of books. And I mean *full*. There are rows and rows of bookstores filled with stacks of books, shelves of them, filling entire walls. Streetlamps light the alley, making all the covers glow in the night.

Harabeoji didn't necessarily love to read, but he was the smartest man there was. At least, that's what he always said about himself. He learned from the people he met while cooking, from history, from life and world experiences. Umma would always scoff a bit when he'd say stuff like this, but I believed him. I still do.

He may not have loved all books, but he loved a good cookbook. Didn't matter what cuisine, what language. He liked to learn from them all.

"I want to get the sound of flipping pages," I tell Yena as we enter one of the shops. "To capture all the times we'd read cookbooks together."

"That's a sweet memory," she says. "Did you make the recipes together too?"

"Oh yeah. He taught me everything I know about cooking," I say. "He ran a restaurant for a long time, which he passed on to my parents. I'm hoping I can cook there one day too. It'd be cool to carry on all the things I learned from him."

"That's special." She smiles. "I can hear how excited you are when you talk about it. I bet that would make your grandpa really happy."

I smile back, but there's a certain heaviness I feel at her words. If only Umma and Appa could see it the way Yena does. By the time they finally let me in the kitchen, will Harabeoji even know how significant it is or what it means to me? Will he even be around?

"Do you think it matters if the sound is from an actual cookbook?" I ask, pushing the thought as far away as I can and moving deeper into the store. I run my hand along the spines on the shelf. "You wouldn't be able to tell, would you?"

"Maybe not you and me," Yena says. "But a true cookbook lover might be able to hear the difference."

"Right."

I keep looking. I find some cookbooks, but they're wrapped in plastic so I can't open them. Finally, I find one that's free to flip through. I get the recording device, fumbling with it in one hand while thumbing through the book with the other until Yena comes over to help me. Our fingers brush lightly as I pass her the book. It feels like sparks dancing on my skin, and I don't let go as quickly as I should.

I press record. She holds the book close to the microphone, opens it, and lets the pages flutter.

Suddenly, the edges of my vision blur. I blink, trying to clear it, but when I look at Yena, I see two of her, standing side by side. Only it's not seeing double, not quite. The two Yenas are different. One is the Yena I know, focused on flipping through the cookbook. And the second looks like a younger version of her, thumbing through a textbook with a bored expression on her face. She looks up and, even as a kid, she is unmistakably so Yena, her sharp, fox-like eyes lighting up as she slams the textbook closed and says, "All done!"

I close my eyes and shake my head, and when I open them again, the second Yena is gone and my vision is clear again. Teenage Yena stares at me.

"Lucas? Are you okay?" she asks.

"Yeah. Fine. Did you say we're done?"

"I didn't say anything. But we are at the end of the cookbook."

"Oh. Okay."

I turn off the recording device and shake my head again. My eyes are going bad. I should get them checked out. I'm not sure what it means that I'm seeing and hearing things, but I have been feeling a bit off ever since the migraine. Maybe I need a full-body checkup.

"You should come home," Umma said over a video call

the other day. I made the mistake of telling her about the migraine and she'd been calling me every few hours since then to see how I was feeling.

"I told you, I'm better now," I said. Harabeoji and I were in the middle of watching a reality show on TV where celebrities go camping around Korea. I excused myself to take the call in his room. "All I needed was some sleep."

I wasn't lying. I did feel about 90 percent better, though sometimes I found myself zoning out and feeling groggier than usual. Umma didn't look convinced.

"Hold on, your dad wants to speak to you," she said. There was a shuffling sound as she passed the phone to my dad.

"Lucas! Why are you not taking care of yourself over there?" For some reason, Appa doesn't seem to understand how to hold a phone when you're video-chatting someone and all I can see is his forehead.

"I am taking care of myself," I said. "It's just a migraine. I used to get them a lot, remember?"

"But he hasn't had one in years," Umma's voice said off-screen. "I think he's under too much stress being in Korea."

"Ya, don't be stressed!" Appa exclaimed. "Why are you stressed?"

"I'm not stressed."

"Is it because of your grandpa's condition?"

"No. It's fine."

"I knew spending that much time with Harabeoji would

only upset him," Umma said. She's lowered her voice, but I can still hear her because apparently, neither of them know how phones work. "We shouldn't have let him go."

Annoyance flared through me. Harabeoji is *her* dad and she was talking about him like he was nothing more than a bother. "I have to go," I said flatly. "Harabeoji and I are doing something."

"Make sure to get lots of sleep and stay hydrated," Umma said, taking the phone back.

"Okay," I said, and then I hung up before she could say any more.

Back in the living room, Harabeoji was flipping through the channels. "Hi, Lucas. Just looking for something for us to watch." He paused on the camping show, squinting at the screen. "This seems fun. Should we try this?"

If I am feeling weird because of stress, I don't blame Harabeoji. It just means I haven't been managing it well. I tuck the recording device away and pull out my phone now, making a quick to-do list on my Notes app.

Make doctor's appointment.
Get eyes checked.
Maybe try downloading a meditation app?

"Want to sit down for a bit?" Yena asks, looking worried. I nod and we walk out of the bookstore, sitting on the patio out front where stacks of manhwa are tied together in tall bundles. I don't want her to worry about me, and I don't know exactly how to explain what just happened either. I still feel a bit dazed. My brain hurts. I'm tired of thinking. So I don't think at all, and instead, I rest my head on Yena's shoulder, closing my eyes.

At first, I feel her shoulders tense in surprise. And then she relaxes, adjusting her height to match mine. "Sleepy?" she says.

"Just tired from the run," I say. "Okay if I rest here for a minute?"

"Sure. First minute is free, but after that I charge."

I laugh, eyes still closed. "That's fine. I'll pay. Tell me again about how I saved you earlier."

"Hmm. Did I say that?"

"Yeah. I think you said I was your hero or something too?"

"Now that I really don't remember." She laughs. It feels good to hear her laugh.

I open my eyes and look down at our palms both pressed against the edge of the patio, so close to each other that if I reached over just a little, my fingers would touch hers. I can still feel the warmth of her hand as we ran into the pojangmacha, how she didn't let go right away, how I didn't either. It felt like the most natural thing in the world. *Love at first sight? Or something like it?* My hand inches toward hers.

And then my phone rings and we both jump.

I grab my phone from my pocket. It's Umma calling me. I consider not answering, but I don't want her to think that something terrible happened to me. With how worried she's been lately, she'll probably jump to the worst conclusion.

"Sorry, I have to get this," I say. Yena nods and I answer the call. "Hello?"

"Lucas? Hi. I think your dad and I are going to need you to cut your trip short and come home early."

I sigh. Not this again. "I already told you that I'm fine. I don't need to come home early."

"No, no. Not because of you. Because of us."

My stomach drops. Now I'm the one imagining the worst-case scenario. Appa's health is acting up. Umma had an accident. The restaurant burned down. So did our house. "What do you mean? Are you okay?"

"Yes, we're fine," Umma says. "But the restaurant is really struggling. Our staff has been dropping off one by one. We had another one quit today and it's nearly down to just Appa and me."

Okay. I take a breath. No fires, no accidents. At least that's a relief. "Why is everyone leaving? What about Joe Ajusshi? And all the new hires at the start of the summer?"

"Joe Ajusshi is our last man standing. He's the only reliable one. All the new hires have completely turned over." Umma sighs, and I can almost see her pressing a hand against her forehead in stress. "It's hard to find good help these days. And we've been having a lot of issues with the fridge lately. It may be on its last legs. We could really use all hands on deck over here."

The words hang between us.

Leave Korea? Now? When I still haven't gotten Harabeoji into the recovery study? And what about Yena? I glance at her. She's pretending not to listen to give me privacy, but of course she can hear everything I'm saying. We just met. Is it already time to say goodbye?

"Can I call you back?" I ask.

I know that's not what Umma wanted to hear. "Okay," she says, tired. "I'm sorry, Lucas. I wish I didn't have to ask you this. I really did want you to have a good time on vacation."

"I know, Umma." The guilt in her voice only makes me feel more guilty myself. "I'll call back soon, I promise."

We hang up. I look down at my phone, at a loss for what to do. This was not part of my plan.

"Want to walk?" Yena asks, sensing my mood.

"Yeah. That sounds good," I say.

We start walking and at first, it helps to move, but then my brain goes into overdrive. I can feel the control slipping from my grasp and I keep going around and around in circles in my mind, trying to figure out how to get it back.

I need to get out of my head. I turn to Yena. "What are your parents like?"

"My parents?" she says, thinking it over. "Well, my dad is lovely. He's a gardener. He's kind and funny and treats me like a friend. When he's around, that is." She rolls her eyes. "I'm still waiting for him to call me back. It's been a while."

"Does that happen often?"

"Only when he's started dating someone new. My parents are divorced and my dad loves love. He'll drop everything for a woman when he's head over heels." She shrugs. "I'd be worried that something happened to him, but this isn't the first time he's gone MIA like this. As for my mom . . ."

Yena stops, looking up. I follow her gaze. There's a big archway above us that says Busan International Film Festival and I realize we've wandered onto BIFF Square. I remember seeing it on Samchon's list of recommendations. The festival happens here every fall.

"I didn't know there was a film festival here!" Yena exclaims. "I love movies."

"Really? Me too," I say. "My childhood dream was to be a director."

"I know."

"Huh?"

She blinks and then gives me a quick smile. "I didn't finish my sentence. I mean, I know, right? I wanted to be a director too. But my mom thought going into film wasn't such a good idea. I bet she wishes I stuck with it now though. She'd be happy if I had some kind of goal."

"You were about to tell me about her," I say.

"I'll tell you another time. Come on, look at this!"

She waves me down the street and I follow her. And

slowly, I do start to get out of my head. I stop thinking about my parents and the restaurant and all the things I don't know how to respond to, at least for now, long enough to look at the handprints of famous actors and actresses pressed into the street, long enough to focus only on the food stalls that stretch before us.

We share fried mandu, the dumplings burning our tongues, and ssiat hoddeok, seed-filled pancakes, cinnamon spilling over our fingers. I record the sound of sizzling oil, the chatter of the crowd, and tell Yena about the meals Harabeoji used to make, the people he used to entertain, and she tells me about all the movies she used to reenact with her stuffed animals at home: *Titanic* in her bathtub, *Spider-Man* with her toys hanging from the ceiling with strings of floss. I wonder if she knows that she's giving me exactly what I need right now—space to breathe—and I can't help but think that if I were to collect sounds of my own life, I would want to capture the echoes of this night, of Yena's laugh, and of BIFF Square in July.

It makes me think.

I've only been capturing memories that I know of Harabeoji. But he had a whole life before he became a grandfather, even before he became a father. What about those sounds? Would he want to remember them?

I want to ask him, but by the time I get back home, he's already asleep. I make a note to talk about it with him in the morning and nod off on the couch moments later.

The water meets me.

The nightmare starts as it always does, with me swimming in the dark. I'm looking for something, maybe the shore, but I don't see it and the more I search, the farther it feels. And then suddenly, my legs feel heavy. More than heavy. There's something pulling me down.

I gasp, the water lapping over my head, submerging me.

I need to live. I need to fight this. I need to survive till the morning and ask Harabeoji all the things he wants to remember.

But the water is too strong. Panic grips my chest and I shout, but only bubbles escape my lips. This is it. This is the end.

"Lucas!"

I gasp, startling awake. Samchon is standing over me, hands on my shoulders from shaking me awake. "Nightmare?" he says.

"Yeah."

"Here, come have some water."

I sit up on the couch, sweat beading my forehead, and then I follow Samchon into the kitchen. He must have just come home from work. He still has his tie on, his shirtsleeves rolled up to his elbows. He pours me a glass of water, sets it on the table, and I drink. It helps calm my nerves just a little.

"Your mom would probably kill me for asking, but want

something else to go with that?" Samchon opens the fridge, holding up a bottle of makgeolli.

"Um, sure," I say.

Samchon grins and sits next to me with two small bowls, pouring us both some rice wine. He's right, Umma would definitely disapprove. But thinking of Umma makes me think of her asking me to leave Korea early, and that makes me push her to the very back of my mind. Samchon and I clink our bowls together and drink.

The makgeolli is tangy and strong and slightly sweet. It takes a second for me to get used to, but by the next sip, I think I like it more.

"Your mom told me about the restaurant," Samchon says, loosening his tie.

So much for leaving Umma in the back of my mind. "Yeah," I say.

Samchon gives me a sympathetic look. "She feels bad for relying on you so much."

I sigh. "I don't want her to feel bad. And it's not like I don't want to help. I care about the restaurant too." I look into my bowl, swirling the makgeolli around. "It's just a lot sometimes. I feel like it's all we talk about. Or how constantly worried she and Dad are about me."

"Well, you know, those are the two most important things in her life. The restaurant and you," Samchon muses. "I know it must be tough for you, but selfishly, a part of me is happy that's the case."

I raise my eyebrows. "Happy?"

"Mhm. I never had a knack for the cooking thing or the restaurant business. But your mom, she took after Harabeoji in that way. I know how hard she works to keep up Lim's Kitchen as his legacy." He gets a look in his eye, a mix of sadness and pride. "We talked about it once after the diagnosis. She said she knows that one day, Harabeoji won't remember all the recipes he made, but she wants to make sure that all the people who eat it through her kitchen will remember it forever."

"She's never said anything like that to me," I say, surprised. Ever since the diagnosis, I felt like Umma avoided talking about Harabeoji or her feelings about his condition. She just seemed to throw herself deeper into restaurant work. I guess now I know why.

Maybe if I knew sooner, it would have been something we could have bonded over. Maybe she'd understand more why I want to work in the kitchen. Maybe it's not too late. I've always just told her it's because I like to cook, but hearing the way Samchon describes it strikes a chord in me. *Legacy.*

Samchon chuckles. "It was a rare moment of vulnerability. As for you, well, it wasn't easy for your parents to have a baby. And when they finally had you, you were born so early you almost didn't make it. But you did and that made you their miracle. I agree that they could worry a lot less about you now, but I'm happy you're here for them to worry about. I kind of like having a nephew."

He grins, topping off his bowl and mine, and I can't help but smile back. I like talking to Samchon. Nothing he said has changed anything about the situation, but I feel better somehow, like he's taken a load off my shoulders. Not only that, but he's reminded me that Umma might be Umma, but she also has her own story even if I don't know much about it myself.

Speaking of stories . . . "Samchon, what do you think Harabeoji would want to remember from his childhood?" I ask.

"Childhood? I'm not sure. He never talked too much about it. But I know he grew up in Damyang."

"Where's that?"

"Probably about a three-hour drive from here, give or take?"

That's not too far. It could be a day trip. "Do you think Harabeoji would want to go?"

"To Damyang?" Samchon says. "I suppose I've never asked. Why? You want to see where he grew up? Take some photos to help jog his memory of the place?"

"Something like that," I say.

Samchon pauses. "You're a good kid, you know that, Lucas?"

"Sure," I laugh, taking a drink.

"No, seriously. I wish I spent more time with my dad when I had the chance. Asked him more questions. I was so focused on work, and with me living here and him living overseas with your mom, it just never really happened. It all sounds like excuses now, doesn't it?"

"You could still spend time with him. He's not gone yet."

"I suppose you're right." He grows thoughtful for a moment and then nods decisively. "I have this Saturday off. How about the three of us take a little trip out to Damyang?"

"Seriously?"

"Yeah."

"That'd be great!" Maybe it's the makgeolli that makes me say the next part, but before I can think too much about it, I say, "Can I bring a friend?"

"You have friends in Busan? Sure. We have room," Samchon says. He raises his drink. "Here's to having more time."

"To more time."

We cheers.

SOUND

THE VOICEMAIL
14 YEARS OLD

"Hi! It's me. Meet me at blue hour. You know where."

He followed the voicemail, riding his bike to the spot. Their spot. A grassy hill behind the playground, mostly empty now because the sun was setting. He squinted in the bright light as he parked his scratched-up bike, hanging his helmet off the handlebars.

She arrived moments later, skidding in on her own bike. "Hi. I was scared I'd miss it today."

"Nah. You're right on time."

He sat on the grass and she took a spot next to him, lying down to face the sky, arms outstretched. They watched the sun sink behind the mountains, coloring the clouds a soft, hazy pink.

She lifted her thumb and closed one eye, trying to cover the sliver of the moon in her vision. "It looks so small from here, doesn't it?"

"Yeah. Imagine how much smaller we must look to the moon."

"Tiny. Insignificant. Makes you wonder if we even matter, huh?"

He lay down next to her. "So. Blue hour?"

Blue hour. He knew it was code for when she wanted to talk. Not just talk like normal talk, but talk like when you're on the phone at 2:00 a.m. or sitting around a campfire watching the embers burn down, wrapped in blankets, knowing that whatever you say, your secrets are safe. But they didn't need to stay up late or have a fire to talk like that. They just needed their code.

She lowered her hand, resting it on her stomach. "Do you know why this is my favorite time of day?" she asked.

He shook his head. She'd never said.

"It's when the sky is most in love with itself. Look. It gets to be all the things at once. Day and night, bright and dark, bold and quiet. It doesn't have to hide or be just one thing. It can be all the things."

She turned to look at him. "I feel like I can be that with you."

He smiled. "Same."

"Is that all you have to say? I try my best to be a poet and you say 'same'?"

His smile faltered. "Um, I mean . . . me too?"

She laughed. "Okay. Whatever. I know in Lucas words that means a lot."

He breathed a sigh of relief. Because she was right. It

did mean a lot. *She* meant a lot, so much that he didn't know how to say it, wasn't even sure how to understand it. He just knew that he liked having a place that was theirs, a time of the sky that belonged to the two of them. He liked how she made him feel and that they could talk about anything.

And they did. They talked about anything and everything, from school to friends to the growing distance she felt with her mother, the stress he bore from his parents leaning on him more and more at work. He wondered what it would be like to reach out his hand and touch hers. She wondered the same. Neither of them did, but whenever either of them shifted slightly, their elbows brushing together or the toes of their shoes leaning against each other, they felt the same flutter in their bellies.

But soon the sky grew dark and it was time to go home. It was the only downside of blue hour, that it lasted so short.

"Hey," she said, standing up her fallen bike.

"Yeah?"

She wanted to tell him one more thing she loved about blue hour. It was because she loved the image of the rest of the city slowing down, getting ready to sleep, while she was here running to him. *Meet me at blue hour,* she wanted to say, *I'll be waiting for you.*

But she chickened out. She didn't want to sound silly. And what about the nightclubs, the graveyard shifts, the places in the city that came to life at night? It was a romantic image she had, but probably not so accurate. Besides, she knew that in all likelihood, he would be the one waiting for her. Sigh. Being poetic was hard.

So she just hopped onto her bike and said, "Race you," and they tore off into the night, streetlamps beaming.

11

YENA

"Well, well, well, look who it is," I say, folding my arms across my chest.

Dad's sheepish smile fills my laptop screen where I have our video chat open on my desk. "I know. I'm sorry. I've been meaning to call." He presses his hands together. "Forgive me, Yena Bean?"

I sigh. "What's her name?"

"Whose name?" he says innocently.

I give him a pointed look and he clears his throat.

"Her name's Alice. She's a librarian. You'll love her, Yena. She's smart and she's fun and she makes her own ice cream. You love ice cream!"

"Yes, because enjoying a universally beloved dessert is the same as loving your dad's new girlfriend," I say, looking at my fingernails.

"Yena . . ."

"Dad . . ."

This is usually the part where we lock eyes in a staring contest, with him looking at me apologetically and me giving him the silent treatment for approximately five minutes before I cave and forgive him. After that, we'll be good again like we always are, until the next time his love life takes up all his attention.

I shift in the awkward silence, about to give in when he says, "Come on, Yena, please don't be mad. I want to hear how you're doing. And how you started running! That's great, by the way. I'm proud of you."

Wait. Have we really not talked since I sent him that photo of me in my running shoes? I glance at the suitcase under my bed where the shoes are locked up, right where I left them after I swore off running. That feels like ages ago. So much has happened since then and Dad wasn't there to listen to any of it, even with all the emergency texts I've sent him.

I look at his familiar face on the screen, and for the first time, I don't want to let things go so easily and pretend I don't care. If I really want to try to get that old part of me back—the part that connects, the part that actually feels everything instead of being frozen in time—I have to start by being honest.

"But I am mad at you, Dad," I say. "You weren't there for me when I was telling you I needed you. And this isn't the first time. You know it isn't. This happens every time you start dating someone new. And it's not that I'm not happy for you and Alice and her homemade ice cream. I just want you to remember that I'm still here too."

A mix of emotions cycles across Dad's face. Surprise, sadness, shame, remorse, back to surprise. "Yena, I'm so sorry," he says. "I know how I can get, and I know that it can be annoying, but I had no idea how much it affected you."

"I guess I never said anything," I say. My voice comes out steady, but my knees are shaking under my desk. "But I'm saying it now because I want you to know."

"No, I'm glad you did. That's something I should know, and something I should have picked up on myself a long time ago." The cycle of emotions slowly comes to rest somewhere between shame and remorse. He looks me directly in the eye, as best as he can through the screen. "Thanks for telling me."

I smile at him, feeling a weight lift off my shoulders. My knees stop shaking. He gives me a watery smile back. "Dad! Are you crying?" I say.

"I just wish I could give you a hug. Why are you so far away?" he says, sniffing.

"Well, are you ready to hear what I've been up to?"

"Please."

I take a deep breath. "I saw Lucas. He's here in Korea and he doesn't remember who I am."

Dad blinks, his tears instantly drying up. "Come again?"

I start at the beginning with the mixtape and tell him everything that's happened since, all the way up to the call I got from Lucas this morning asking me if I want to go on a day trip to Damyang with him and his family this weekend. I go into more detail than I did with Danielle about how I've been feeling, the thoughts I've been having, and it's strange to say the whole story out loud, like I can't believe it's even real. Strange, but therapeutic.

The whole time, I watch his face carefully to see if he betrays any signs of having known all along that Lucas erased me. But Dad's eyes only grow bigger and bigger as I talk and by the time we're caught up, he's just staring at me, open-mouthed.

"I should have called sooner," he says.

"You really should have."

"I really, *really* should have."

I hesitate, not wanting to ask but knowing I have to. "Dad? Did you know? About Lucas's erasure?"

He puts a hand over his heart. "I truly did not."

The relief I feel is palpable. I didn't realize how scared I was that maybe he knew this whole time and he was just keeping it from me. It would have changed everything I knew and trusted about our relationship.

"Have you talked to your mom about it yet?" he asks tentatively.

"Not . . . yet."

With each passing day, I feel like it only gets harder to find the right time, the right way, the right words to talk to Mom about Lucas. She's so busy that it's hard to catch her, but every small chance I do get, I always make excuses.

She's stressed. Every morning I step out of my room to see more balled-up pieces of paper littering the floor, remnants of her late-night research notes with dirty mugs stacked higher and higher in the sink. If I didn't know any better, I'd think she was trying to set a new world record. Or *there's not enough time.* I've typed up more than a dozen Google Calendar invites to reschedule our teatime only to delete them before sending, hoping for a magical perfect opportunity to present itself on its own instead. It hasn't and if it did, let's be honest, I'd probably let that pass me by too.

"Do you want me to bring it up with her first?" Dad asks.

I pause. Do I? It would be easier to have him call her, to hear the information relayed through Dad than to hear it from Mom directly. It's always been easier to talk to Dad. But I shake my head. "No. I need to do it myself, face-to-face. I will soon."

He nods. "All right."

"So. What do you think about all this?"

I don't know why, but I feel nervous waiting for his response. Is he going to call me sadistic like Danielle? Or selfish for hanging out with Lucas when I know that it could hurt him? Maybe he's going to tell me to move on, but I'm not ready to hear that either.

He sighs deeply, propping his elbows up on his desk and

resting his chin against his fists. "Listen, Yena. I remember how devastated you were when Lucas moved away and cut the friendship. I know I've said this before, but you were never quite the same after that. And that was really hard for me to watch. It's like you convinced yourself that you stopped caring about anything. And I'm not trying to pin this all on Lucas. God knows we had a lot of things going on at home and there were a million things I could have done better to be there for you. But all I'm saying is, I saw your world revolve around this boy once and shatter. I don't want to see that happen again. You do what you have to do, but just be careful."

I look down at my keyboard, run my finger along the edge of my laptop, blink back the sudden tears pricking at my eyes. Why am I crying? I wipe them away with the back of my hand. Maybe it's the feeling of having someone care about you this much and say so. Or maybe it's just the tenderness of his words.

Did my world revolve around Lucas before? Does it now? I can see why Dad might worry that it's true, but I know in my gut that this is about something much bigger than just Lucas. I'm figuring things out for myself, and this time, I'm determined not to shatter.

"Thanks, Dad. I hear what you're saying."

"I trust you," he says. "And look, I want you to update me on everything. I mean it, especially about how Damyang goes. I'll be better about replying, I promise."

"I have to see it to believe it," I scoff, but I'm smiling. I know he means it, and that's a good start.

He blows me a kiss through the screen. "Love you, Bean."

Lucas said we're going to Damyang with his grandpa and uncle. The night before the trip, I lie awake in bed, wondering what it will be like to see Harabeoji again. Will he recognize me? What do I do if he does? What do I do if he doesn't? Even if he remembers who I am, I'm certain he'll know that Lucas erased me, so I'm guessing he wouldn't say anything anyway. But what if? What if what if what if?

As for Lucas's uncle, I've never met him, but Lucas described him on the phone as "nice. Easy to talk to. Very loud." This turns out to be exactly accurate.

Lucas's uncle honks the horn as he pulls up in front of my apartment where I'm waiting outside, early Saturday morning, to meet them for Damyang day. He rolls down the window.

"Lucas, you didn't tell me that your friend is a model!" he exclaims in Korean.

"Sorry about him," Lucas says from the back seat, lowering his window as well.

I laugh, looking through the window and bowing my head. "Annyeonghaseyo."

And then I see Harabeoji, sitting in the passenger seat,

and the breath catches in my throat. The sight of him is surreal, like having one foot in the past and the other in the future. He looks just as I remember him, but older, more tired, fragile. He was always so sturdy and bursting with life in the way you can only be when you've lived it to the fullest. His eyes turn to me and my heart pounds in my chest.

"Annyeonghaseyo," I say again. My Korean's been getting better, but it feels rusty again with how nervous I feel. "I'm Bae Yena. Nice to meet you."

Something like familiarity passes across his face, but it disappears just as quickly as it came. "Geurae, geurae," he says, accepting my greeting. He gestures toward the back seat. "Hop in."

I get into the car. Lucas smiles at me and I smile back, but it feels strained. Even if Harabeoji's response was what I anticipated, I can't help but wonder if it's his condition that's made me foggy in his mind, or if he's pretending for Lucas's sake. Either way, it's more emotional than I was expecting and I have to swallow the lump rising in my throat.

"All right, off we go," Lucas's uncle says cheerfully. He turns to Harabeoji. "Why don't you play some music for the ride?"

"Music? Sure." He runs his hand across the buttons and dials on the dashboard. "Which is the one for the radio again?"

"You have your Bluetooth connection, remember?"

"Bluetooth?" Harabeoji says. "What is that?"

Out of the corner of my eye, I see Lucas's face fall and I get the sense that it's not because of age that Harabeoji doesn't know what Bluetooth is. Lucas's uncle clears his throat and turns on the radio.

"Actually, I haven't listened to the radio in a long time. Good idea," he says.

The music plays and we drive on.

"You know, I grew up here, but it's really changed since then. I wish I could show you how it used to be. You'd say wow! Is this the same place? I don't think so."

Damyang is a small town that takes us about three hours to get to. We stop for stretch breaks and snacks, and when we arrive, our first stop is Harabeoji's old neighborhood. Or at least, what Lucas's uncle thinks Harabeoji's old neighborhood is based off an address book he found. I'm not sure what was there before, but now there are tall apartments and modern-looking playgrounds that I suspect weren't there when Harabeoji was a child. But even though it all looks different, there's something about being in Damyang that gives Harabeoji a new spring in his step, a liveliness in his voice. As if his body recognizes his hometown even if his eyes don't.

"Your grandmother and I met in middle school here,"

he says to Lucas. "She was the smartest girl in our grade."

"Is the school still around?" Lucas asks. "What was it called?"

"Oh, it was so long ago," Harabeoji says.

"I have it in the address book!" Lucas's uncle says.

We visit the school, still standing, and afterward we go for lunch and eat ddeok-galbi, a Damyang specialty. I notice Lucas recording little snippets of the day. Harabeoji's voice, the sound of children yelling, gathered on the field for a summer sports day, meat patties sizzling at the restaurant where we sit clustered around one table, metal chopsticks tapping against rice bowls.

He's trying to capture it all for his grandpa, and I can't help but feel emotional again. There's a chance that nothing will ever come from the Memory Recovery Study. Even if he gets in, what if things don't work out the way he hopes they will? I'm not sure how Lucas feels about the setback in the study that I told him about, but it seems like he hasn't given up on his plan just yet. If anything, he seems to be holding even tighter to whatever hope he has that he can fix this.

I'm so lost in my thoughts that I almost don't hear my phone buzzing in my pocket until Lucas nudges me. "I think you have a call," he says.

"Oh, sorry." I glance at the screen.

Dr. Bae.

Weird. Mom never calls me. "I'll be right back," I say, excusing myself from the table.

I step out of the restaurant, answering the call. "Hello?"

"Hi, Yena. Where are you? I finally have a full day off and thought we could catch up, but you're not at home."

Her voice sounds weary, as if she hasn't slept in days. I haven't had a shift at the clinic since that day with the reporters, but from what I've seen on social media, the protestors have not let up. If anything, they've only multiplied in number.

"Are you doing okay?" I ask carefully. I don't want to bring up the protests if she doesn't first.

"Work's just been busy," she says. She doesn't expand.

"Okay. Well, I'm actually not in Busan right now. I'm in Damyang."

"What?"

"Damyang? It's a small city—"

"I know Damyang. Why are you in Damyang? That's a bit far from Busan for you to go off on your own."

Her tone is sharp, worried, the tiredness grating to the surface. Whoa. I was not expecting this from her. Since when does she care where I go? "I'm not alone," I say. "I'm with my friend and his family. They invited me to come along for a day trip."

"What friend?"

Now it's my turn to prickle. "Just a friend," I say stiffly.

I can almost feel the suspicion in her silence. But there's no way I'm going to bring Lucas up like this, not over a phone call when he and his family are literally sitting steps away from me.

"I would have appreciated you telling me before going on a trip," she says. "You're still a teen and I'm your mother."

"It's not like I ran off without anyone knowing. I told Dad," I say, exasperated.

It's the wrong choice of words. Her silence grows so frigid I can feel it through the phone.

"Okay. Well, if you told your dad, then that makes it all fine. I'll see you when you get back," she says curtly, and before I can say another word, she hangs up.

I stand there, staring at the screen. I'm so frustrated I want to call her back, reach through the phone, shake her until she understands. *You don't get to be mad at me!* I want to yell. *Not when you're the one who's been keeping things from me for years.*

The restaurant door opens, the bell jingling above it. "Hey," Lucas says, stepping outside. "Everything okay?"

"Yeah. It was just my mom checking in," I say, and all of a sudden, the fight drains out of my body and I start to cry.

Alarmed, Lucas rushes over and holds me in his arms. My instinct is to pull away, to not let him see me like this, but he's so warm, so safe. I bury my face into his shoulder and let myself cry. They're frustrated tears, angry tears, sad tears. Why can't she just be there for me the way I need her to be? Why do I always end up disappointing her?

Finally, the tears subside, and I step back, hiccuping. "Sorry. It's really nothing," I say, mortified. "Look at your shirt."

He looks down at the wet splotch on his shoulder. "It's fine."

"I'm a mess."

"You . . . are maybe a mess. But at least you're not bleeding this time. Remember when we first met? I never knew jogging could be so hazardous."

His face is serious, his voice deadpan. I laugh. But what I really want to say is, when we first met, I was wearing a No Face costume. You were Totoro ordering popcorn. You and your grandpa invited me to sit next to you because you got a size too large. We found out we went to the same Korean school, and from there? It was years of moments like this, of you holding me when I was crying about my mom moving to Korea, saying why can't she stay with me? Why does she have to go so far away? She could open up her clinic here. She could stay. But she's choosing not to. She wants to leave me behind.

I want to say I was a mess, I was always a mess, and I can't even count how many T-shirts of yours I've cried on. You wouldn't say much, never did, but you always had a way of making me laugh with your serious expressions, of holding me until I felt okay again.

I don't say any of that even though I want to. But something in the height of my emotions makes me want to take a chance, so before I can regret it, I say, "Hey. Does the term blue hour mean anything to you?"

He smiles quizzically. "Isn't that the window of time right after sunset?"

I nod, heart racing.

It's said that sometimes, memories are triggered in the strangest of ways. Contrary to popular belief, there's no such thing as a memory bank or one place in our brain where all our memories are stored. I learned that at Sori. Memories are more like constellations where each star represents a piece of the whole: a star for how it sounds, a star for how it smells, a star for how it looks. The stars are scattered across the sky much like these pieces of information are stored in different parts of the brain, but seeing one can naturally cause you to trace the whole constellation.

That's how Sori Clinic erases memories. They target a core star to find the constellation. But I can't help but think that maybe it's still there, burning in the sky, just waiting to be looked at again when the right reminder comes along. *Please*, I think, looking at Lucas. *Remember me.*

"Is that when we should be back in Busan? So you don't get home before it gets too dark?" Lucas guesses.

The hope snaps away. Me and my wishful thinking. "Yeah," I say. "That's right."

"We should get back inside, then," Lucas says, holding the door open for me.

I walk back into the restaurant, blinking away my disappointment. What was I expecting?

As if it could be so simple to bring back a star.

12

LUCAS

Before we leave Damyang for the day, Samchon wants to take us to the most popular spot in town: the bamboo forest. Harabeoji has never been before since it opened after he moved away, but Samchon insists that we can't miss it after coming all this way.

"When are we ever going to get the chance again?" Samchon says, buying us tickets at the booth to enter the forest. "We have to take this opportunity. Isn't that right, Yena?"

"Oh, definitely," Yena says. "Thanks for letting me tag along today. I had a blast."

Samchon and Yena chat animatedly as we walk into the forest, Harabeoji and me following behind. They get along great just like I thought they would. Yena laughs, all traces of her earlier distress gone. Or at least, hidden. I can still feel the way she cried into my shoulder like she was completely defeated. She said it was nothing, but I'm guessing it had to do with the phone call with her mom.

A dull pain throbs in my head and I wince. Harabeoji notices and asks, "Everything okay?"

"Yeah," I say. "Just a headache." I've had it ever since lunch. I really should make a visit to the doctor soon.

Damyang Bamboo Forest, as it turns out, is huge. Towering bamboo trees stretch toward the sky, sprawling out as far as the eye can see. They look almost ethereal, the way they're swaying in the breeze. I lift up my recording device, capturing the sound of the wind in the trees. I'd like it if Harabeoji could remember this.

The forest is filled with well-maintained dirt paths, and we pick a trail to walk along. "She's sweet," Harabeoji says as we stroll at a leisurely pace. Samchon and Yena are already almost out of eyeshot with how much farther along they are. "It's nice that you've stayed friends for so long."

"Who? Yena?" When he nods, I laugh and say, "I feel like it's been a long time too, but we've only known each other for a few weeks."

"Weeks? You mean years," Harabeoji says. "I can't think of two closer friends. Though if you ask me, I'd say you had a crush on her from day one." He chuckles.

I frown. I'm never quite sure how to respond when Harabeoji starts talking about things I don't understand, but it's usually in the realm of him forgetting. I've never heard him recount things that never happened. Do I correct him or just go along with it?

"I know your parents aren't the biggest fans of her, but I'm glad you stuck by her side," Harabeoji says, patting my arm.

"Why don't Umma and Appa like her?" I ask despite myself. I shake my head. Get a grip, Lucas. This isn't actually real.

His brow furrows. "I suppose they think she's not a very good influence on you. There was that time when you almost—"

"Hey! Slowpokes!" Samchon's voice yells from farther down the trail. "Are you coming?"

"Yes!" I holler back. I turn to Harabeoji. "What were you saying?"

But his attention has already moved on. "What incredible trees. Where are we right now?"

"We're in Damyang Bamboo Forest, Harabeoji."

"Damyang! Did you know I grew up here?"

My head throbs again and I stumble on the trail, accidentally dropping the recording device. Harabeoji bends down to pick it up, turning it over in his hands.

"What is this?" he asks, handing it back to me.

I hesitate. I could tell him what it is and say I've been getting into sound design as a hobby. But maybe this is my chance to bring up the study with him again. Ever since Yena told me about the mistake in the Memory Recovery Study, I've been thinking more about how to talk about it with Harabeoji. It's not great that that happened, but it is a trial program. I can't expect everything to go perfectly, and I still feel like the potential benefits outweigh the risk in the long run. But I know Harabeoji won't see it that way.

Still, with Umma and Appa wanting me to come home sooner than later, I need to start convincing him to get on board. At the very least, if I do end up having to leave, I can pass all the preparation I've done to Samchon, and Harabeoji can still enroll in the study when there's a spot. It's not the best plan B, but it's still a plan. I just have to get him to agree.

"I'm collecting the sounds of your memories," I say. "So you can remember them if you forget, or you can strengthen them before that can happen."

Harabeoji stops walking and stares at me. The wind blowing through the bamboo trees makes it sound like the forest is whispering, like a restless crowd waiting for his reaction.

"How are sounds supposed to help with that?" he asks.

"It's preparation for Sori Clinic's recovery study. They need the sounds to work with your memories."

His face grows stormy. The whispering of the trees gets louder. "Lucas. Are you telling me that you've enrolled me into this study?"

"Not exactly." I can't look him in the eye so I look at the dirt path beneath my feet instead. "The study is full right now. I just put you on the waitlist and started doing the prep work."

"Well, you can stop because there's no way I'm doing it," Harabeoji says sternly.

I look up at him and see the stubbornness in his eyes.

My head pounds and I grit my teeth, irritated by the pain.

"Can't you at least think about it?" I ask. The words come out harsher than I mean them to, less patient. "You're the one who's always telling me to leave doors open. Why are you being so closed-minded? This could literally be a saving grace for you."

He shakes his head, his stubbornness turning to steely resolve. "No, Lucas. I don't want this. End of discussion."

End of discussion? Harabeoji never shuts me down like that. Ever. He starts walking again and I stare at his back, moving away from me.

"How do you even know what you want?" I shout after him. "Can you even trust your own mind anymore?"

He stops and I instantly regret it.

Why did I say that?

How do I take it back?

I can see Harabeoji's shoulders rise and fall with a deep breath and then he keeps walking without turning around. I press my lips together, trying to stop myself from crying, and then I follow along behind him.

The wind quiets and now all I can hear is the silent judgment of the trees and my heart pounding in my ears to the beat of my own shame. *Regret. Regret. Regret.*

Samchon proposes an early dinner before we drive back and takes us to Guksu Geori, literally Noodle Street. Close to the bamboo forest, it's a street right by the river lined with noodle stalls. Usually, I would be excited by something like this. I love noodles. But as we sit down at one of the outdoor tables with bowls of thin noodles swimming in myeolchi broth, all I can think about is my conversation with Harabeoji and I can't taste a thing. I can't even bring myself to look at him or Samchon or Yena, I feel so ashamed.

Harabeoji doesn't say anything either, and I know Samchon and Yena can tell that something is wrong. Yena catches my eye across the table and gives me a cautious smile. "You okay?" she mouths.

I try to smile back but my face won't cooperate. Instead, my frown only deepens as I remember what Harabeoji said about Yena in the bamboo forest. How we've been friends for years.

Was he mistaking her for someone else? Or just confused? I would chalk it up to his condition, but Yena's question from earlier comes back to me. *Does the term blue hour mean anything to you?*

I feel a strange wave of déjà vu, like I did that day I saw her at the crosswalk. Should it mean anything to me? Am I the one missing something here?

Harabeoji stares out at the river, where there is a group of friends riding pedal boats in the shape of cars. They look like enlarged bright children's toys bobbing in the water. "I want to go for a walk along the river," he says, standing up.

"Now?" Samchon looks up from his bowl, noodles halfway to his mouth. "We're still eating."

"I'm done."

"Well, just wait until we're done too so we can go together."

But Harabeoji is already on his way. "I won't go far. You can keep an eye on me from the table if you're worried."

Samchon frowns. "All right then. Don't go too far."

Harabeoji shuffles away, hands behind his back, with Samchon keeping one eye on him and one eye on his food. My stomach twists. Harabeoji always goes on walks when something is on his mind. Our conversation must still be weighing heavily on him too.

It's strange. He used to be the most independent person I knew. He could do five things in the kitchen at once without ever losing focus or missing a beat. But now he needs his own son's permission to go on a walk? I don't think I'll ever get used to how much everything has changed.

I turn back to my food, picking listlessly at the noodles as Samchon and Yena finish their bowls down to the last drop of broth. Harabeoji used to make guksu just like this for me, I recall sadly. He'd go through phases of trying out a recipe and we'd eat the same thing for days. There was the guksu phase. The jjajangmyeon phase. He even went through a milk tea phase after trying it for the first time and getting inspired to re-create it at home.

How could I have said all those terrible things to him?

I'm thinking about going to join him on his walk to

apologize when, from farther down the river, I hear a loud *splash!*

I'm standing before I even realize it, chopsticks clattering from my hands. Samchon's head whips toward the water.

"Where's Harabeoji?" he says, jumping to his feet. "He was there just a second ago."

"I don't see him," Yena says, worried.

There's splashing in the river, someone trying to get to the surface. Samchon is already running, and I am too.

Or at least, I think I am.

In my head I am.

But in reality, I'm frozen to the spot, eyes fixed on the water, mouth dry. I can't move. I can't speak. The fear that falls over me is so big, so heavy, it feels like a spear flung straight through my body, pinning me in place.

Harabeoji is drowning, I think, *and there's nothing I can do to stop it.*

The panic spirals in my gut and wraps around my lungs. I can't breathe. Neither can Harabeoji. I try to move, move, *move,* goddamn it! But I'm shaking too much to take a single step.

And then Yena is in front of me. "I'm going to put my hands on your shoulders, okay?" she says. Her voice is soft but firm. I nod and she places her palms on my shoulders, inhaling deep, and then exhaling. "Follow me on the next breath."

When she inhales again, I follow, and when she exhales, I do the same. We do it again. And again. The pounding in my ears gets a little quieter. The shaking in my hands a little more stable.

"You're fine. You're safe," Yena says. "And you know what? So is your grandpa."

"What?" I say.

She points toward the riverbank, where Samchon is standing with Harabeoji, slightly obscured by a tree. In the water, one of the boys who was riding the car-shaped pedal boat is swimming to the dock while his friends laugh and shout out to him.

"Can't believe you fell out trying to take a selfie!"

"Nearly gave us all a heart attack."

I collapse into my seat. "Harabeoji's fine? He didn't fall in?"

Yena shakes her head. "No. He didn't fall in. Here." She passes me my cup of water and I take a sip. "How do you feel?"

"Just . . . a little embarrassed." He was literally standing behind a tree. I should have looked more closely instead of freaking out like that. Why did it have to be water, of all things? I shudder, thinking of my recurring nightmare. It's silly that my stress dream has somehow turned into a real-life phobia.

She smiles, her face brightening. "Hey, now we're even."

"Even?"

"Yeah. You're embarrassed now and I was embarrassed before when I got snot all over your shirt."

"You didn't get it *all* over."

"Let's not get caught up in arbitrary details when I can still see the stain on your shoulder, Lucas," she says seriously, and then she brightens again. "My point is, our embarrassment cancels each other's out. So neither of us have anything to be embarrassed about."

"I guess that's one way of looking at it," I say, smiling weakly.

Samchon and Harabeoji are walking back from the river. Samchon waves his hands over his head and yells, "He's okay!"

Yena smiles and waves back, running over to join them.

In the forest, Harabeoji also said something else strange. That my parents think Yena is a bad influence on me. I know it can't be true because there's no way anyone could ever think that. Right now, it feels like she's the only thing helping me stay tethered to the ground.

For good measure, I take one more deep inhale. One more deep exhale. And then I run to join them too.

SOUND

THE FILM REEL
13 YEARS OLD

It's nice to be appreciated. I would know. I haven't gotten that kind of attention in a long time.

That is, until they found me. The boy and the girl stumbled into the AV room by chance. "We shouldn't be here," the boy said nervously. "We're only supposed to stay on the floor where our classrooms are, remember?"

"Relax, it's break time. No one's going to know," the girl said. "I just want to see what else is in this building, other than Korean school. Wait—what's that?"

"What's what?"

"That!"

"Don't scare me like that, Yena, I have no idea what you're talking about."

She pulled the cover off me, dust flying into the air, and gasped. "It's one of those old-school film reels!"

"What? No way!"

The nervousness in the boy changed to excitement as he ran over to join her. He looked at me in awe and for the first time in a while, I felt beautiful again.

"So cool," he said.

"Do you think it still works?"

"I'm not sure. I have no idea how these things work."

Somewhere in the building, a bell rang. The boy looked regretfully at the door.

"Break's over," he said.

She didn't move, still entranced by my beauty.

"Yena," he said.

"Okay, okay, I'm coming." She reluctantly hauled the cover back over me, but before she did, she leaned in and whispered, "I'll come back."

And she did, the very next week, with the boy by her side. And they came back the next week, and the week after that. Each time, they stayed a little longer past the bell. At first, they attempted to fix my broken parts and get me to work like I used to. But it's been a long time since my glory days, and I was afraid they'd grow tired of me and leave me alone again.

But to my surprise, they stayed. They eventually gave up on trying to fix me, but they would come into the room, take off my cover, and play a sound from their phone that was remarkably similar to the one I used to make. The *tick tick tick* of my breaths that I wasn't sure I'd ever hear again.

And then, the best part. They would bring out a computer and play a movie on it, almost as if pretending that it was coming from me.

I can't remember the last time I was this happy. I missed

watching movies so much and watching them again with these two was like getting a second chance to live.

But all good things must come to an end. After several weeks of skipping class, their teacher found them and called their parents. The girl came back one more time by herself to say goodbye.

"I'm going to miss you," she said, gently touching my side. "But Lucas's parents got really mad that he was skipping and he promised he wouldn't do it anymore. I think they blame me for it. I'm going to try and be better too, but just so you know, I'd way rather be here with you and Lucas than in class."

She blew me a kiss and put my cover back on for the last time. After that, I didn't see them anymore. But our time together gave me light again and sometimes, when I'm alone in the room, I can still hear the cinema playing in my head.

13

YENA

It's been a day.

By the time Lucas and his family pull up in front of my apartment to drop me off, I feel like all of us are at low battery. The drive back to Busan was mostly quiet. Still, as I get out of the car, I catch Lucas's eye and he gives me a smile. It's tired and I can tell he's in his head about stuff, but it's also knowing, like we're sharing something that belongs only to us. I haven't seen that smile in a long time and my heart stutters as I say goodbye, waving at the car until I can't see them anymore.

I hesitate outside the apartment building. Will Mom be home? She said she had the day off today. I should go in and talk to her if she is. I start to head inside and then turn back around, waffling.

What am I going to say to her? I should think about this first. Have a list of things I want to talk about in case I forget or clam up on the spot.

Or maybe I should just go with the flow and see where the conversation takes us. I don't want it to sound too rehearsed. I head back toward the door and then turn back around again. Or maybe it's fine if we don't talk at all. We've come this far, haven't we? What's a little more silence between us? Or maybe—

I stop pacing. I can see someone walking across the apartment lobby through the glass front doors. Someone who looks a lot like Dr. Bae.

Oh God. It *is* Dr. Bae.

I quickly duck behind a bush as she exits the apartment. Luckily, she's talking on her phone and doesn't notice me. "Yes, Tony, I know it's my day off," she's saying as she starts walking down the sidewalk. "But there's a new theory I just thought of and I need to process it out loud before I lose it."

I wait until she's farther away, turning left around the corner, and then I follow her.

I keep a solid distance between us, close enough that she's in my line of vision but far enough away that I can make a quick escape if she happens to turn around. I can't hear what she's saying to Tony on the phone, but I can see her gesturing a lot with her hands, so absorbed in whatever she's saying that I suspect she might not even realize I was there if I were walking right next to her.

At first, I think she's going to the clinic because of course she would be. The only two places she ever goes are work and home. But then I realize we're going in the opposite direction. I hang back, watching as she crosses the street and walks into a roller-skating rink.

A roller-skating rink?

Well, this is unexpected.

Right as the traffic lights are about to change, I hurry across the street and follow her inside.

Stardust Roller Rink feels like stepping into another world. There's a lively, retro vibe here with pink and purple lighting, K-pop blasting from the speakers, and a sparkly disco ball hanging from the ceiling. People of all ages spin and stumble and dance around the giant rink, laughing, clinging to each other's hands, lost in the music by themselves. One wall is lined with circular neon clocks showing different times around the world: Busan, Paris, Kuala Lumpur, Lima. I do a double take when I see the clocks. They look a lot like the pink one that Mom has at home, the only personal touch in the whole apartment.

"Would you like to rent a pair of skates?" a girl in a collared varsity shirt that says Stardust Roller Rink across the front asks me in Korean.

"Oh, no, thank you, I'm not here to skate," I say. I pause. Why am I here? I followed Mom by impulse, my body moving before my brain could really think too much about it.

I spot her now, in the middle of the rink, skating like she's been doing it her whole life. She's not on the phone anymore. Instead, she looks more relaxed than I've ever seen her, rolling to the beat of the music with a content smile on her face.

I sit down on one of the benches along the side of the rink and watch her. Who is she? She's almost unrecognizable here. Not hyperfocused Dr. Bae or absent Mom. Just somebody who loves to skate.

I'm so lost in the strangeness of it all that I don't even realize almost an hour has passed until Mom steps off the rink and spots me. She freezes, the tension returning to her shoulders, and I immediately regret following her. Whatever this space means to her, I clearly shouldn't be here.

"Yena?" she says. "What are you doing here?"

"I'm . . . skating," I say, unconvincing.

She looks at the sandals on my feet, with no roller skates in sight.

"Okay, no, I'm not," I admit. "I saw you leave the apartment, and I followed you because we need to talk. I just didn't want to interrupt you when you seemed so . . ."

Happy. That's the word that comes to mind, the thing that made her look so different on the rink. She doesn't look like that at work. Or when she's with me.

". . . in the middle of something," I say instead. "So I was waiting here for you. Sorry."

"Oh." She looks awkward, standing there in her skates. "That's fine. No need to be sorry."

She collects her shoes and sits down next to me, taking off her roller skates in silence. This close, I can see the dark circles under her eyes, the matted, unwashed hair that she's tried to hide in a ponytail. She's so obviously exhausted, and I feel guilty for snapping at her on the phone earlier. She already has enough going on without me adding to her stress.

"Did you have a good time in Damyang?" she asks, her tone clipped. "You don't have to tell me if you don't want to. I'm sure you've already talked about it with your dad."

My guilt immediately evaporates. I was going to play nice, but if she wants to pick up right where we left off, then fine.

"Come on, Mom. I'm sorry I didn't tell you about Damyang. I honestly didn't think you'd notice or care."

"Why did you think I wouldn't notice or care?" she asks, not looking at me as she changes into her shoes.

"Seriously? I'm not exactly your first priority."

She sighs. "You know how busy it's been with the new study. If you knew what we were dealing with at the clinic, you'd understand why I've had to put in extra hours these days."

"It's not that I don't understand," I say, irritated. Why does she have to be so defensive about everything? And why does she have to turn it around and make it sound like it's my fault for not knowing enough? "Trust me, Mom, word gets around. I know the study is struggling. It's kind of hard not to notice the reporters and protestors harassing me when I leave work."

She looks up at me at that, her mouth falling open. "They harassed you?"

"They had questions. They seemed to know I'm your daughter."

In a flash, she's back on her phone, business mode. Her fingers fly across the screen. "That's unacceptable. I'm taking care of this right now."

"Taking care of what?"

"If these reporters think they can bother you—" She breaks off, staring at me. "Why didn't you tell me about this sooner?"

"Mom, please! Are you even hearing what I'm saying?"

I don't mean for my voice to come out as loud as it does, but she startles and so does the group of teenagers sitting on the bench next to us, tying up their roller skates. I feel like we're going around in circles and I'm losing my patience.

What are your parents like? Lucas's question comes back to me and I can't help but wonder how I would answer if I was completely honest, holding nothing back. As much as I know Mom, I don't really *know* her. I've always admired her work as Dr. Bae, her dedication, but as a mother? I don't know how to talk to her. I don't even know how to be myself.

"You haven't been there. And I'm not just talking about the past few weeks in Busan. I mean in my life," I say. "I know work is important to you and you always have a million and one things going on, but it's like you forget I even exist sometimes. And I'm your daughter! Doesn't that count for anything?"

The group of teenagers next to us rolls out onto the rink. The music is still bumping, the disco ball flashing, the pink lights dancing across Mom's face as she presses her lips together, eyes shiny like she might be holding back tears.

"It counts," she says quietly, almost to herself. And then, louder, "Of course it counts."

I can feel the shift between us, the tentative openness. We've never talked about this before. About her moving away right after the divorce, about me and her and what we really think of each other. It would feel so good to get everything out in the open, to actually say what's on my mind.

But I can't. I can't talk about these things with her, not until she answers my biggest question.

I want to know. I don't want to know. The push and pull, the coil of fear that's been knotting in my chest, growing tighter and tighter at the very idea of facing the truth—I breathe it down, exhale it away just long enough to see right through it. *I need to know.* It's now or never.

"There's something I've been wanting to ask you, but I haven't had the chance," I say.

"What is it?"

I reach for the right words, lose them, settle for the ones I manage to grasp. "Do you remember my childhood friend Lucas Pak?"

She stills, and in that moment, my stomach drops. She knows what I'm about to ask her. She knows that he erased me. She knows everything I knew she would know this whole time but was too scared to hear out loud for fear that it would consume me, and it does. I can't stop my hands from shaking.

"I found his mixtape," I say, not looking away from her eyes, afraid that if I do, I'll lose the guts to keep going. "He erased me from his memories. Did you know about that?"

"Yena," she says, but she doesn't say anything else.

I swallow hard. "Were you the one who did his erasure?"

Say no, I demand inside my head. *Say you didn't do it.* It's wishful thinking, but I can't help it.

She doesn't say no. Instead, her eyes fill with an expression I've never seen on her face before. Regret.

"I'm sorry," she says.

"Why didn't you tell me?" At this, my voice breaks. Not just my voice. All of me. Every part. I'm falling to pieces. She turns her face away as if she can't bear to look at me any longer.

"Patient information is confidential," she says quietly.

My heart crumbles.

Mom was still around when Lucas and I became friends. Even after she moved to Korea, she would see him when she came to visit. Then after he disappeared, she would listen to me on the phone, crying, "Where did he go? How can someone just leave like that?"

"Nothing is forever, Yena," she'd say, trying to comfort me. "Some people are meant to be in your life for just a moment. It doesn't make what you had any less special."

She knew what he meant to me, and she knew where he went. But she kept it from me all these years. Expecting something to be true is one thing, but having to accept it as reality is so much colder, so much uglier.

"I went to Damyang with him today," I say. "He's in Korea to try and help his grandpa into the recovery study. I met him outside Sori Clinic."

She winces, but strangely, she doesn't seem as surprised as I thought she'd be to hear that Lucas is in town. "Did you tell him what you know?"

"Of course not. How can I?" I remember my feeble attempt from earlier today to jog his memory, my attempts in all our days together to try to piece together the holes in my story. But no matter how much time I spend with Lucas, I don't think he's ever going to be able to give me what I'm looking for. "Do you know why he did it? Why he erased me?"

Now that I've started asking all my questions, I can't seem to stop. How can I be so angry at her and, at the same time, so hopeful that she might be the one to save me from the spiral in my mind? *Tell me there's a reason. Tell me what I did that was so wrong.* The memory of me and Lucas sitting outside the ice cream truck flashes through my head. *Is it because I wanted too much? Because I was too much?*

She opens her mouth, closes it again, and then says with

a note of finality, "It was a long time ago. I see a lot of patients and sometimes the details get blurry."

I can't tell if she's saying the truth, but whether she is or not, she's done speaking and any feeling I had of wanting to hash things out withers away. I don't want to talk about anything with her ever again. I don't want to trust her with anything ever again. I can feel my walls go up, my defenses higher than they've ever been.

"I guess that's it, then," I say. And then I stand, walking out of Stardust Roller Rink as fast as I can.

The warm evening air envelops me as soon as I step outside. I didn't realize how strong the AC was in there. I'm shaking. Or maybe that has nothing to do with the temperature. Mom follows me outside, reaching for my arm. "Yena, wait," she says.

I turn, letting her stop me, and despite myself, I'm hopeful again. "What?"

"I don't know what right I have to give you advice as a mother, but please trust me when I say this. Don't see him again. It will only hurt both of you in the long run."

That's not what I wanted to hear, but I know she's right. I've known ever since Tony warned me that my being around Lucas could hurt him. And it has. The migraine at the fish market, how confused he seemed in the book alley, and even today in Damyang. I know he didn't want to show it, but I could tell something was off from the way he would grimace and touch the side of his head when he thought no one was looking, like he was trying to relieve a headache. I knew all of that and still, I chose to keep seeing him, to keep putting him at risk.

And me? I know she's right about me too. As much as I've tried to ignore it, my heart breaks a little more each time I see him. How much longer until there's nothing left of me to break?

"If you can promise me that you won't see Lucas again, I can get him a spot in the Memory Recovery Study," Mom says.

My eyes widen. "Is that a bribe?"

"No. I'm asking you to do a hard thing, and I'm offering you something in return." She squeezes my arm once before letting go. "Think about it. Okay?"

Think about it? How? I don't even know how to begin wrapping my mind around anything that's happened this summer.

What am I supposed to do now?

* * *

Me:

Hey. Super random, but would you be able to meet up today?

Me:

There's something I need to talk to you about.

Somehow the next morning, I find myself pulling out the suitcase from under my bed, unlocking it, Mom's running shoes right where I left them. I stare at them for a long moment, and then I take them out, put them on, lace them up. When I look in the mirror to tie my hair, a reluctant runner looks back at me.

I told myself I would never run again, but when I messaged Danielle asking if she can talk, she said she goes for a run every Sunday morning at Taejongdae and my best bet to catch her is to tag along. So here we are. Second chances.

It's a long bus ride to get there and I sit with my head against the window, listening to Lucas's mixtape. The now familiar sounds of popcorn machines and film reels carry me all the way to the cliffside national park, where I see Danielle by the entrance, stretching.

"I didn't even know you were a runner," I say, approaching her.

"You never asked, did you?" Danielle says, straightening up. She gives me an amused smile. "Surprised you actually decided to join me."

I realize this is my first time seeing her outside work. It's a bit strange, like seeing one of your teachers outside school hours, but it's also kind of cool. I follow her lead, stretching.

"I'm getting the impression that you might be some kind of super runner," I say, watching how confidently she warms up. She's even wearing the kind of clothes you see in fitness ads. "I just want you to know that I am not that."

"Trust me, I remember the way you looked when you jogged to work that one time," she laughs. "I'll go slow. Ready?"

"Nope, but let's do this."

We start running. Even though it's quite early in the morning, the park is already starting to fill with people, a mix of locals and tourists. There's a long trail shaded by trees that wraps around the ocean, leading all the way to a cliffside view and a lighthouse. As far as running goes, this is a pretty nice place for it, and true to Danielle's word, she goes at a pace that I can keep up with.

"So what did you want to talk about?" she asks.

It takes me a minute to settle into a rhythm where I can run and talk at the same time. I don't know how she makes it look so easy.

"I had this conversation with my mom yesterday," I say between breaths. "About Lucas."

"Oh?"

I fill Danielle in on everything Mom said and the deal she made me at the end. "If I don't see Lucas anymore, she can get him a spot in the study. But I don't know what to do," I say. I hardly slept at all last night thinking about it, only to conclude that there's no way I can make this decision by myself. I need to talk to someone. Someone who might understand what it's like to be on the side of the forgotten. "I was wondering, if you're comfortable with it . . . could you tell me more about your dad and how things were after he erased your mom?"

It's hard to predict what Danielle's response will be. She's not exactly the most emotive person, but she has surprised me before with how open she can be.

"It's not easy," Danielle says, looking straight ahead as she runs. "The situation is obviously a little different than yours. Dad couldn't erase everything about my mom. Before the erasure, he cleared out all their photos together, all her stuff from the house, anything that would make him think of her, but he couldn't get rid of me and my siblings. And how could he explain our existence if he wiped her out completely?

"From what I know, he had his memories erased so that he couldn't remember anything specific about her, but he knew he had children with somebody who was no longer in the picture. So it was this really weird thing where we had to pretend she didn't exist anymore because to him, she didn't, even though we're living proof that she did."

She looks lost in her thoughts, physically here in Tae-jongdae with me, our footsteps keeping time with each other, but mentally back at home in Irvine, reliving these moments. "I was so mad when he got rid of all her stuff. So mad. I went to the thrift store where he donated a bunch of her clothes and bought back everything I could find. But none of it smelled like her anymore."

We approach a lookout point and she slows down. Relieved, I gratefully collapse onto a bench to rest. She sits down next to me, and we both stare out at the ocean. The water here is so alive, the waves crashing against the rocks in every shade of blue imaginable.

"Do you still talk to him?" I ask. "Your dad?"

She stretches her legs out in front of her, absentmindedly tapping the toes of her shoes together in thought. "A little. It's still hard because it feels like there's this big chunk of our relationship that's missing, that we can never talk about. And he's not an easy person to be around. Just because he erased my mom doesn't mean he was able to erase his grief. The body still remembers even if his brain doesn't, and he gets confused and angry a lot."

I nod. That's like what Joanne said about her sister. How she may have erased the things that hurt her the most, but the hurt doesn't necessarily go away.

Danielle sighs. "Even though I do keep in touch with him, it doesn't mean I forgive him. I don't know if I ever can. Things will never be the same."

"I see," I say.

I'm not sure if it's the ocean view or the fresh air, but sitting here with Danielle, it feels so easy to talk to her. All the stuffiness that's usually between us at the clinic is gone and I really appreciate how honest she's being with me, especially about something so personal. It makes me wonder if I could ever fully forgive Lucas, what it would look like for me to have a relationship with him knowing that he'll never remember the things I do. Could I do it? Do I want to do it?

"My mom thinks that if I keep seeing Lucas, I'll only get hurt," I say. "And I know she's right. It's hard to be with him, but I also feel like myself again for the first time in years. That's not nothing, is it?"

"It's not nothing," Danielle agrees. "But it will wear on you eventually, remembering things that he will never and always having questions about that."

"What if I tell him everything?" I ask. It's a thought I haven't been able to shake since Damyang. I'm not just a stranger to him anymore. He trusts me. He knows me, at least who I am to him now. He might believe it if I told him the truth, that we once knew each other, that we have a history longer than he knows.

"You could," Danielle says. "But if you're triggering side effects just by being around him, what do you think would happen if you tell him everything?"

Honestly, I'm not sure. I would have to ask Mom or Tony what would happen. But even if there aren't extra risks, is the truth something I want to burden him with? He erased me for a reason. He probably doesn't want to remember me.

"I wish he could know without me having to say

anything," I sigh. "Can't he just have a moment of epiphany? Like in the movies when people with amnesia get hit in the head or struck by lightning and suddenly remember everything?"

Danielle laughs and then falls quiet. She gets to her feet, extending a hand to help me up. "Come on, let's keep running. We're almost at the lighthouse."

We jog, and this time, I don't talk. Not only because I literally, physically cannot run and speak coherent words at the same time anymore, but because I'm turning over everything in my head.

Lucas is back in my life, and this time I can keep him. But I know I'll always be wondering. I've spent years pretending that I'm fine, that I don't care, but I know I'll never be able to let go of the questions I have and the hurt that I carry, not if I'm reminded of it every time I see him.

God, I wish there was another way. But if I say goodbye to him now, he can get Harabeoji into the Memory Recovery Study, which was what he always wanted. And this time when we part ways, he'll remember me. I'll be the girl he met that one summer, the one who helped him gather the sounds.

It makes me ache, the bittersweetness of it. But then we turn a corner, jogging down a set of stairs until we come face-to-face with the sea, the sun, the brilliant white lighthouse standing guard on the shore. For a moment, the chaos in my mind quiets as I follow Danielle to the cliffs, where we climb onto the rocks to get a better view of the water. Maybe running's not so bad after all.

The wind whips against my face and here, near the wildness of the ocean, the summer humidity doesn't feel so hot.

14

LUCAS

Dear Mr. Lucas Pak,

We would like to inform you that a spot has opened up in Sori Clinic's Memory Recovery Study and you are next on the waitlist. If you are still interested in participating, please fill out the forms and waivers below, and follow the link to book your appointment. Thank you.

Best,
Joanne Kim
Receptionist, Sori of Us Clinic

I sit at Samchon's kitchen table and read the email a dozen times—no, more than a dozen times. I can't believe it. I got Harabeoji into the study.

The first thing I think to do is call Yena. I'm so excited I nearly drop the phone. It rings and rings and goes to voicemail.

"Hi, it's Lucas," I say in a rush, unable to keep the smile from my voice. "Call me back when you can. I have some news I want to share. And . . . I'd love to see you."

I hang up, not even overthinking about how she might interpret that last part and whether it sounds cringey. I haven't seen her since Damyang, which was already a few days ago, and I want her to know that I've been thinking about her. I want her to know that I want to see her face.

My phone rings and I immediately answer, thinking it's Yena calling me back. "Hello?"

"Finally, Lucas! Where have you been? Is everything okay?"

It's Umma. My excitement deflates.

"Hi, Umma. Sorry, I've been busy. I wasn't ignoring you on purpose."

Only I kind of was. I haven't wanted to think about going back to Edmonton early so I've just conveniently had my phone on silent whenever Umma called, texting her instead to say I'm fine and that I'll call her back later.

"Have you thought about what I asked?" Umma says. She sounds tired, more tired than I've heard her in a long time. I think about what Samchon said, about how the restaurant is Umma's way of carrying on Harabeoji's legacy. I want to carry that with her, but I can't leave now, not when I just got this email.

"I've thought about it a lot actually and, Umma, is there any way I can stay longer? I know you and Appa need me, but I can't leave quite yet. Maybe with everything going on, this is a good chance for you two to take a break as well? Close the restaurant for a little while to recharge?"

"Take a break?" she says, bewildered. "Lucas, what are you talking about? We can't close the restaurant to run off on holiday. This is the worst time to do that."

"I'm not saying you need to close for a long time. Just a week or even a few days to get some pressure off your shoulders. When's the last time you even went on holiday? Or took a day off?" I press. "Maybe the restaurant's not the only thing breaking down. You need to rest."

She sighs deeply and when she speaks again, her voice is gentle but patronizing. "I hear what you're saying, Lucas. Gomawo, for thinking of me and Appa. I do appreciate it. But now is not the time to take a break. We have bills and staff to pay and we could really use your help."

Now is the moment I could tell her about the study. That I got a spot for Harabeoji and that maybe, just maybe, this could help his condition more than anything else. But something stops me.

My fight with Harabeoji comes echoing back to my mind. The harsh things I said, the way he kept on walking without turning back. We haven't spoken about it since. If I'm making plans about his future, I should tell him first before telling anyone else in our family.

So instead, I say, "I just don't know when I'll be able to have this kind of time with Harabeoji again. I don't want to cut it short. And I've met a friend here too. We've really been getting along, and she even met Samchon and Harabeoji the other day."

"Oh?" Umma says, curious. "That's nice. How did you meet?"

I pause. How do I answer that question without bringing up the study? "She's originally from Vancouver, actually," I say, choosing my words carefully. "She's here working at her mom's clinic for the summer. It's called Sori of Us Clinic. Have you heard of it?"

I float the name to see how she might react. Would Umma have strong feelings about memory tampering too? But all I hear on the other line is silence, and I think I've lost her.

"Hello? Umma?"

"I'm here." Her tone is oddly tense.

"Did you hear what I said?" I ask, uncertain about the shift in mood between us. "About Sori Clinic? They study memories."

"Listen, Lucas," she says, the earlier gentleness in her voice gone. "I'm sorry, but I think we've been patient enough with you. We need you to come home. Tomorrow."

"Tomorrow?" I exclaim. "You can't be serious." I was supposed to stay with Harabeoji for another month. Even if I were to end up leaving early, I didn't think Umma meant *this* early. It all feels way too sudden.

"The day after tomorrow, then. That's more than enough time to get ready to leave," she says. "I'll be rescheduling your flight today."

"Umma, you can't—"

Before I can finish my sentence, she hangs up. I call her back, but she doesn't answer. I'm stunned. What just happened? It's not like her to be so rash. Or to end a call without giving me a list of things to be careful about.

I drop my head into my hands, frustrated. How could she do this? Just when Harabeoji gets into the study, she goes and changes my flight?

The study. I lift my head and hurry to Harabeoji's bedroom door. I knock. If Umma is serious about this, I have to get a move on. There's still my plan B to pass the study on to Samchon, but it's not ideal with him working full-time. And he'd just be one more person to convince before we can get things going.

I have to do this. And fast.

When Harabeoji doesn't respond right away, I crack the door open. He's sleeping soundly in bed, but he stirs awake at the sound of the door.

"Taehoon? Is that you?" he croaks.

"No, Harabeoji, it's me, Lucas," I say.

Harabeoji has been napping a lot these days, even more than usual. I don't want to interrupt, but he's already sitting up, gesturing for me to come in.

I sit at the foot of his bed. "Can I get you anything? Water? Food?"

"No, no, I'm okay," Harabeoji says.

"Okay." I felt so rushed a second ago, but now that I'm

sitting here in front of him, I find myself hesitating. How do I bring this up? How can I convince him after how terribly our last conversation went?

Before I can say anything, Harabeoji beats me to it. "I'm glad you're here, Lucas, because I just remembered there's something I want to apologize to you for."

"Apologize? To me?" I say.

"Yes. For what happened in Damyang," he says. "I'm sorry for shutting you down in the middle of our conversation. That wasn't right of me."

"What? No. I'm the one who should be sorry," I say, taken aback. "I said some terrible things. I regretted it as soon as I said it."

"I know you did." He smiles kindly. "We're both sorry. And we both forgive each other?"

"Well, that depends," I say nervously. "Of course I forgive you. But I think you're going to want to know something before you forgive me." I take a deep breath. Here goes nothing. "I got an email about the Memory Recovery Study at Sori Clinic. A spot opened up for you. And I really, really think you should consider taking it. I know you don't trust them, but at least go to the first appointment to see what it's about. You might change your mind, right? Isn't it worth giving it a shot if there's even a small chance that it can help you?"

I speak fast, saying everything before I can chicken out, but I'm so scared I can't look him directly in the eye.

I have no idea how he's going to respond and I don't want to fight again.

Harabeoji takes my hands in his. I didn't even realize that mine are clenched in fists until he smooths them out, unfurling my fingers. "Relax," he says. "What did I tell you about holding your hands like this?"

"That I'll break the eggs," I say quietly.

"That's right." He mimes rolling an egg in my direction, just the way he used to do when we were in the kitchen making gyeran jjim. "You've always held on to life too tightly. You'll only get broken eggs if you keep doing this. Sometimes you just have to let things be and stop trying to control everything."

He gently tilts my chin up to look at him. His eyes are clear. Harabeoji has good days and bad days, and lately it's felt like more bad than good. But right now, he looks as sharp as I always remembered him.

"I'm not doing the study, Lucas."

"Please, Harabeoji," I say. "I need you to do this. You're only going to get worse and I can't—I don't—I don't want to lose you."

But I can tell by the resolve on his face that in this, he won't change his mind. The desperation I've been clinging to that I can fix this and somehow change the future is dissolving in front of me and I grasp on to his hand as tightly as I can instead.

"I don't want you to go," I say, my voice breaking.

"I'm here."

"I want you to stay with me."

"I'm here."

"Aren't you scared?"

"I'm so scared," he says, and his eyes grow shiny with tears. "I'm scared of the way I'll become a burden to my family. I'm scared of the way I won't recognize myself anymore. Will I still be me without my memories? I don't know." He smiles, letting his tears fall. "I don't have the answer to that. I'd like to believe that I will be, but we'll have to see when we get there. But as scared as I am, Lucas, I won't risk an experiment to avoid my future. I've seen what memory tampering does. And to me, it's not right."

"What do you mean you've seen what it does?" I wipe the tears from his face, trying to swallow the lump in my own throat. "When have you done it before?"

"Me? No, I'm talking about you," he says. "I always wished that I could have done something to stop it. To this day, it's one of my biggest life regrets."

I stare at him. "What?"

But he's looking somewhere past me now, the focus in his eyes growing distracted. I can almost see him moving on to another thought, our conversation already slipping away.

"Harabeoji?" I say.

He pats my hand one more time and swings his legs out of bed, putting on slippers. "You know what I think will make both of us feel better? Subak. We have one in the fridge, don't we? We should eat it now. Summer is the best time for subak."

He shuffles out of his bedroom to the kitchen. I follow him, watching as he promptly forgets why he went in there in the first place and begins to prepare a cup of tea instead. I take a deep breath, trying to mentally catch up to the sudden change, and then I get the watermelon from the fridge myself. But my head is still spinning from our conversation.

What did he mean by what he said? Was he implying that I've had my memory tampered with? Because that's what it sounded like.

I think back to our walk in the bamboo forest as I cut the watermelon into triangles. That was strange too, when he was talking about Yena as if I've known her for a long time, long enough that Umma and Appa would have an opinion on her when they've never even met her. Or have they?

I shake my head. Now I'm overthinking. This is all impossible.

But then. I picture Yena's face, the twirl of her hair when she clips it up, the déjà vu I felt when she ran across the crosswalk to meet me.

Does the term blue hour mean anything to you?

When I held her in my arms as she cried, I swore she would be able to feel my heart pounding in my chest, a mix of being nervous at her closeness but wanting her to be closer still. But even in that, there was an undeniable familiarity. Like we fit together. Like we'd done this a hundred times before.

I'm so lost in my thoughts that I accidentally nick my thumb with the knife. I pull back, wincing as blood blooms on my skin. And then, almost like a ghost in my ear, I hear the memory of someone saying, *My first kitchen wound. That makes me a chef like you, right?*

I startle, looking around as if someone might be standing over my shoulder. But there's no one but Harabeoji, rearranging plates in the cupboard, humming to himself as his forgotten cup of tea sits steeping on the counter.

What is going on?

SOUND

THE ICE CREAM TRUCK
14 YEARS OLD

As soon as people hear my music, they know who I am. They chase me down the street, waving their arms to get my attention, wanting me to stop for them. I guess you could say that's just how far my popularity goes. Though admittedly, that day was a slow day. So slow that my driver parked me on a residential street and waited for people to come to me, tired of driving around with no success. Although I'm sure he was just going to the wrong places.

Eventually, a boy and a girl came up to get my autograph. The boy got a Popsicle in the shape of Spider-Man's head and the girl got a chocolate-dipped vanilla cone coated in peanuts. They sat on the curb in front of me and ate, chatting, the ice cream melting down their fingers as the sun beat down over their heads.

The boy looked nervous. Maybe to be in my presence? He seemed like he was gearing himself up to say something to the girl. He turned to her but in that exact moment, she turned to him too. They stared at one another as if surprised to see each other so close and then just as the boy opened his mouth to speak, the girl blurted out, "I think I love you."

His mouth stayed open but no words came out. And then there was a shout from down the street and a group of kids came running to me. My fans! They ran right between the girl and the boy, splitting them up. Cheeks burning red, the girl sprang up from the curb and said, "I totally forgot, I have to go home early today. Talk to you later!"

"Wait!" the boy called out after her, but she was already running.

He sighed, pressing a fist against his forehead. Meanwhile, I was busy handing out autographs. An ice cream sandwich for you, a Creamsicle for you.

After the crowd of kids cleared, the boy was still there, staring down the street where the girl had run away. His Popsicle was long gone and so was she.

"Tough day?" my driver asked sympathetically, leaning out my window to address the boy.

"Something like that," he said. He shook his head. "My parents want to move to Alberta. I haven't been able to tell her, but I was going to do it today."

"Ah. This was a goodbye ice cream."

The boy gave my driver a look. "No. I mean I was going to tell her that my parents want to move, but I'm not going to go. I'm going to stay here with her. I can't leave her behind."

"So then why didn't you say anything?"

"I wasn't expecting her to say what she did." He looked

down the street again and said, so quietly that only I could hear, "I was going to say it first."

Sometimes I still think about the boy and the girl. I wonder if he ended up moving away and if she ever did stop running. There was something about them that made me hope that things would work out. What can I say, I have a soft heart. Every so often, even now, I'll dedicate a song to them as I play my music down the street.

To the girl who said I love you and to the boy who wanted to say it first. This one's for you.

15

YENA

How many times can you say goodbye to one person?

I sit inside Café Daisy, waiting for Lucas. After talking to Danielle yesterday, I decided I would take Mom's offer, but even though her deal was that I won't see him again, I thought I could allow myself one last meeting. After all, the other goodbyes weren't really goodbyes, not for me. This is the only real one I'll get and this time, it'll be on my terms.

Lucas walks into the café, sees me. I wave, my stomach twisting in knots.

"Hey," he says, taking a seat. "Thanks for inviting me out. I was so glad to hear from you."

"Of course," I say. Suddenly, now that he's sitting right here in front of me, I don't know how to do this. I don't know how to say goodbye. I push it off a little longer, nudging an iced latte in front of him. "I ordered this for you. Extra sweet."

"When'd you learn my coffee order?" he says, touched.

"I'm a fast learner," I say. "So, you said over text that you have news?"

"Yeah." He twirls the straw around in his coffee, letting the ice cubes clink together, and smiles. "I got an email this morning saying that a spot in the Memory Recovery Study opened up and I was next on the waitlist. It's Harabeoji's if he wants it."

Wow. Dr. Bae moves fast. "That's incredible! That's what you wanted, right?"

He nods, but there's something hesitant there, something somber. I think about his choice of words. *If* Harabeoji wants it.

"Is your grandpa still not on board?" I ask.

"He's pretty dead set against it," Lucas says. "You were right that time at the fish market when you said I should listen to what he wants. I just thought maybe I could change his mind."

This whole summer, he's been unwavering in his plan, but now he seems uncertain, almost adrift. I know how much this meant to him and it hurts to see him like this.

"I'm sorry, Lucas," I say. "If he does end up changing his mind, you'll have all those sounds collected already. You're one step ahead of the process."

"Yeah, that's true," he says, nodding, but there's a deflated note to his voice. "There's something else I wanted to tell you."

"What is it?" I ask.

"My parents need my help at the restaurant. They're cutting my trip short and want me back in Edmonton the day after tomorrow."

My heart drops. Is he for real? I didn't come here so he could leave me first. I'm the one who's supposed to say goodbye this time. There's also something so final about the fact that he'll be leaving Korea this soon, like it makes it more real that this is the end. Our time together is up and it was too short. It's always too short.

"Oh," I manage.

"I don't want to go. I'm still trying to convince them to change their minds." He's looking at me so intently, a question in his eyes that I can't quite decipher. "But if there's nothing I can do and I have to leave, we'll keep in touch, right?"

He wants to keep in touch. This isn't a goodbye, not for him. Somehow, this makes everything ten times harder. I want to reach across the table, hug him, tell him that I'll never let him go again.

But I know in my heart that I can't. When I got home from my run with Danielle yesterday, I looked at myself in the bathroom mirror, cheeks flushed, sweaty ponytail, clothes sticking to my skin with humidity, and I saw a glimpse of the girl I used to be. A girl just living life and doing her best to take one step forward at a time. A girl doing the thing, no matter how imperfectly, instead of doing nothing at all. Being with Lucas again has reminded me of that girl, but it's also shown me how much I've neglected her, how much I need to start protecting her again. And that means making hard choices instead of ignoring them.

I don't want to do this. Don't make me do this. It's so much easier to let life pass me by, feeling as little as possible. Because when I feel, I feel too much. But maybe it's time for me to embrace that part of myself instead of running away from it. So right now, this is what choosing looks like. This is what embracing is.

I take a breath and give him my best, most convincing smile. "We can try, but to be honest, I'm not that great at keeping in touch. Long-distance friendship isn't really my thing."

"What about long-distance more than friendship?" he says.

I freeze, rooted to my chair. His face is so serious, so open, heart on his sleeve in a way I've never seen before even in all my years of knowing him. I don't know what to say. No, that's not true. I know what I want to say. I know exactly what I want to say.

If it were up to my heart, I'd shout *yes!* I'd get up and take his face in my hands and kiss him right here in this café, and in that kiss, I'd tell him everything I've wanted to say to him for years. We would kiss and kiss until the staff kicked us out and then we would run to the sidewalk and kiss some more. After all, the past is the past. What matters but who we are now?

But it does matter. It matters to me. And as much as I want this, as much as I want him, I'm never going to be able to let go of our history. And I don't want to be the only one who remembers it. If I say what I really want to say, it'll be just as Mom said. In the long run, I'll only hurt myself and I'll only hurt Lucas more than I already have. This is for both of us.

"Lucas, I'm so glad . . ." My voice catches despite myself, and I clear my throat, try again. "I'm so glad we met this summer. You helped me process a lot of things I was going through, more than you'll ever know. But I'm good at temporary. I don't really stick to things. So let's just be happy with the time we had and if we ever meet again one day, I'll count myself lucky."

He looks at me like he knows I'm not telling the complete truth. His eyes search mine, gaze intense, and he says, "Have we met before?"

It catches me completely off guard. "What?"

"Before this summer. Have we met?"

Does he know? Does he remember? Does this change things? Please let it change things.

Now it's my turn to stare intently at him, trying to see what he sees. My heart is racing. Maybe a part of him has started to suspect, to remember. What if I told him everything right now?

You could. Danielle's voice comes back to me. *But if you're triggering side effects just by being around him, what do you think would happen if you tell him everything?*

I twist my hands in my lap. No, I can't take the risk. I know the instructions that patients at Sori Clinic get before they receive an erasure. Destroy all the evidence of the memory you're erasing. Remove as many potential triggers as you can. The mind is a fragile thing. To remember something that's been intentionally forgotten, to recognize that you even got an erasure, can mess with your head. Besides, this doesn't change the fact that he erased me in the first place for a reason, whatever that reason might be.

I won't burden him with this.

"I don't think so," I say. "But I've been told I have one of those faces. Lots of people say they think they've seen me before."

"Oh," Lucas says.

Silence hangs between us. He looks confused, uncertain, sad, and I feel that too, all of it, so much that I think I'm going to burst. I grab my tote from the back of my chair and stand. "Listen, I actually have to head out now. Good luck with everything, okay? The study. The restaurant. Harabeoji. I wish you the best."

This is not how I pictured goodbye, like I'm dismissing him from a job interview. But if I stay any longer, I don't think I'll be able to hold it together. I pause to take one last look at him, to try to memorize everything about his face. The seriousness, the softness, the dusting of freckles across his cheeks. He's still wearing his heart on his sleeve. It looks broken.

"Bye, Lucas," I say before I start crying.

And then I run out of the café and let my tears fall.

* * *

I feel like shit. Worse than shit, really. Dad has been texting me daily since his promise to be better about checking in, asking *How was Damyang? Talked to your mom yet? Everything okay? SOS?* but now it's me leaving him on read.

I don't want to talk about it.

I don't want to talk about anything.

When I wake up the day after my goodbye with Lucas, I already have a plan to call in sick and stay in bed, watching movies and working my way through an entire box of Choco Pie. Danielle doesn't need me. The Memetery is almost done being organized anyway.

But when I call Sori, Joanne picks up and says, "Yena. I'm glad you called. Did you hear Danielle just quit her job?"

I sit up in bed, half-eaten Choco Pie rolling down my blanket. "What are you talking about?"

"She came in this morning to say she's quitting and that she's sorry for not giving earlier notice. I thought you might know something about it?"

"No, not at all," I say. I'm already getting out of bed, trading my pajama shorts for a pair of jeans. "Is that all she said?"

"Yes. Oh, and she did leave a package for you."

A package? "I'll be right there," I say.

I hurry to work, calling Danielle on the way. Her phone goes to voicemail so I shoot her a text.

Me:

Hey did you quit?????

Me:

What happened?

Me:

Is it because I kept getting crumbs in the boxes from eating on them? I'm sorry! I'll never do it again.

Me:

I hope everything's okay.

By the time I get to our building, I'm so impatient that I can't even wait for the elevator. I take the stairs two at a time until I burst into Sori Clinic's front lobby, where Joanne is on the phone.

Without missing a beat, she reaches into a drawer and pulls out a small, brown, rectangular box. She passes it to me, mouthing, "From Danielle."

"Thank you," I mouth back, and then I hurry to the Memotery. On the way, I pass the staff room, which is filled with way more people than it usually is, and to be frank, way more people than its capacity allows. I don't think I've ever seen more than two people in here at a time, but there are at least seven members of the research team in there right now, chatting cheerfully, shoulders squished together as they pass around a bottle of sparkling pear juice. Tony catches my eye through the open door and waves at me, inviting me inside.

"Yena! Come in and join us for a celebratory drink," he says, grinning. "No alcohol during work hours as per Dr. Bae's rules, but this sparkling pear is quite good!"

"What are you celebrating?" I ask.

"Big breakthrough in the study," Tony says. "You heard about the patient whose memory we accidentally erased, right? Dr. Bae had a theory about how to restore that memory and it worked! We just successfully completed the procedure this morning." He leans forward, lowering his voice. "Of course, bringing back memories that are lost to other causes is still a work in progress, but at least we know we can bring back anything we accidentally erase through our own technology. A huge relief, and possibly a big step forward in figuring out other methods of restoration." He raises his voice again, lifting up his drink. "Cheers to that, am I right, folks?"

The other staff in the room all cheers, clanging their mismatched cups and mugs together.

"So, pear juice?" Tony asks.

"I actually have to get somewhere, but congratulations!" I say. And I mean it. That is a major win for the team and for Mom. Even though I'm still mad at her, I'm glad things seem to be turning around for the study. Maybe now the news can report something positive about Sori Clinic for once.

I enter the Memotery, closing the door behind me. The shelves are nearly all organized, the cardboard boxes that were filled to the brim with mixtapes at the beginning of the summer now flattened and neatly lined up against the wall to be recycled or reused elsewhere. It really felt like a never-ending slog, but looking at it now, I can see how much progress we've made.

I sink down on the floor and look at the package that Joanne gave me. There's a Post-it note with my name written on it in Danielle's neat cursive. *Yena Bae.*

I open the box.

Inside, there's a plain white card and a cassette tape labeled *Patient 202.* For a second, I think it's Lucas's mixtape. I gave it to Danielle that day at Taejongdae. Knowing me, I would have probably played it to death for the rest of my life, and if I decided to let Lucas go, I didn't want to be constantly reminded of it. "Put it on the shelf and don't ever let me touch it again," I said to Danielle.

But Lucas was Patient 201. So who's 202?

I open the card first. It reads:

Yena,

I suppose your bad habits rubbed off on me. After I found out you were listening to the tapes (pretty sure that's against confidentiality rules, by the way, but I won't tell anyone), I went and bought a Walkman to listen to them too. What can I say, you got me curious. Anyway, I found this one and thought you might want to hear it. I'm sorry if it burdens you more than it helps. But knowing you, I felt you'd want to listen. Also, I'm sorry for everything that's about to happen next. It was not my intention to hurt you, but I know that it will and I know I'm doing it anyway. I hope you might be able to forgive me one day.

—Danielle

PS In case you need to verify it. 22CactusWrapperJar.

This has got to be the most cryptic thing I've ever seen in my life. I reread the entire note again. I can't make sense of the second paragraph at all. *What's* about to happen? Why would I be hurt by it? And the postscript—verify what?

A foreboding feeling spreads in my stomach. I pick up the cassette tape. The first paragraph about the tape being a burden is a mystery too, but that one I can solve right now. I fumble in my bag and pull out my Walkman, opening it. I don't know what it is she thinks I'll want to hear, but there's only one way to find out.

I stick the tape in, put my earphones in, and press play. The sound of water fills my ears. Water like waves, lapping against a dock. I close my eyes and feel almost like I'm standing on it, trying to keep my balance. There's a splash, the sound of someone diving in. More splashing. More splashing. And then a familiar voice.

"Yena! You fell asleep in the middle of the movie again. This is what you get. Your phone is going to be filled with videos of me when you wake up. Oh, and also videos of you snoring. You're welcome."

My eyes fly open.

What the hell?

"Don't forget about the race you challenged me to at the lake next week," Lucas's voice says. "Remember, loser has to answer any truth or do any dare. And yes, I already know what my truth or dare for you is going to be."

I rip out my earphones and pull them out of my Walkman, throwing them across the room in shock. My head is pounding.

What is this? Why am I hearing Lucas's voice on this tape? Lucas's voice talking to *me*?

He sounds young here, maybe fourteen, but I don't remember this audio at all. What videos are these from? What race at the lake is he talking about?

I rack my brain trying to remember, ignoring the growing pain from the headache spreading across my forehead. It's only natural that I'd forget some of the smaller details of our relationship. Maybe this is just one of those details.

But something in my gut tells me that's not the case. That

there's something wrong here. Very, very wrong.

I grab Danielle's card, my eyes landing on the postscript. *22CactusWrapperJar.*

In case you need to verify it. The password for the laptop.

I hurry to grab it from its spot on the shelf, my hands shaking. I type in the password, scroll to the database. Search up the patient number.

And there it is, as clear on the screen as it was in Danielle's handwriting.

Patient 202: Yena Bae.

16

LUCAS

I have one day left in Korea. Yesterday when I got the email from Sori Clinic, that didn't feel like enough time to do anything. Today, I'm staring at the wall, not sure what I should be doing at all.

What now?

What next?

For all my efforts to stay in control, I've never felt so lost in my life. Things didn't go the way I'd hoped with Harabeoji. And they definitely didn't go the way I'd hoped with Yena.

I don't have any more plans. No to-do list in my Notes app that might change the situation. Still, I fill out all the forms for Sori Clinic and book an intake appointment for later today, almost out of habit, as if doing something will distract me from the fact that I'm out of options now. I know it's pointless. Harabeoji's not going to change his mind, and whether I like it or not, I have to accept the fact that I can't force him to do something that he feels so strongly about.

So I go through the motions, brain in a haze, and I try not to think about Yena because replaying our conversation at the café hurts. I wasn't sure if she felt the same way about me as I do about her, but I wasn't expecting her to say goodbye. Not like that. And I can't help but cringe at the way I asked her if we'd met before. That probably sounded like some kind of last-ditch effort to win her over. Very cool of you, Lucas. Great final impression.

But still. I'm glad I asked because I couldn't shake the feeling, still can't shake it now, that I'm missing something and everyone knows it but me.

My phone rings with an unknown caller. Normally, I'd ignore a call like this, but I'm in such a slump today I answer without thinking.

"Yeoboseyo?" I say in Korean, half expecting a wrong number.

"Hi, is this Lucas Pak?" the person on the other line says in English.

I sit up straighter on the couch, somewhat lifted out of my lethargic state. Not a wrong number after all. "Yes? Who is this?"

"My name is Danielle Flores from Sori Clinic. I have a package to deliver to you. I'm wondering if you can confirm the address I have on your file?"

"Is this for the Memory Recovery Study?" I ask. I think back to the email I received, trying to remember if there was a segment about getting a package. I do recall reading about the equipment needed for the study, but I thought I'd get that at the intake appointment.

"Something like that, yes. Is this the correct address?"

She recites Samchon's address to me. "Yes," I say tentatively. "That's correct."

"Great. The package will be delivered to your lobby in about an hour. Thank you."

She hangs up before I can ask any more questions. I frown, staring at my phone. Just in case, I look up the phone number to make sure there's nothing sketchy about it. It links back to Sori Clinic's website.

Okay, so I guess it's legit. As instructed, I head downstairs after about an hour and, just as she said, there's a small box sitting on the lobby floor with my name written on it. Sori Clinic's full address is printed in the corner. I pick it up, give it a shake. Something rattles around inside, like plastic against plastic.

There's still something a little off about all of this, but there are enough signs that it's safe that I open the box. Inside, there's a cassette tape, a Walkman with a pair of corded earphones wrapped around it, and a card.

I carry it up to Samchon's apartment. Harabeoji's still out with Mrs. Cha for the morning so I have the place to myself to inspect the box.

I open the card first.

Lucas,

I don't know you at all and I wasn't sure if you'd want this, but you'll most likely find yourself reading about it online and connecting the dots. I was given this tape, but after much thought, I feel it should be returned to you should you have questions that burden you more than the answers themselves ever would. It's against my better judgment, but I'm making a call based on my gut. I hope it's the right one.

—Danielle Flores, formerly at Sori of Us Clinic

Danielle Flores, as in the person who just called me?

I look at the cassette tape. *Patient 201*, it says. It dawns on me what this is. A mixtape that Sori Clinic patients use to erase their memories. Why would Danielle be sending me one of these?

Immediately, a suspicion comes to mind and grows stronger and stronger as I open the cassette tape case. I've never used a Walkman before, so it takes me a second to figure out what I'm supposed to do with it, but eventually, I plug the earphones in and hit play.

It starts with wind chimes. Then the *tick tick tick* of a film reel. Waves. I involuntarily wince at that and wait for it to pass. A lawn mower, a kitchen knife chopping, popcorn popping. The music from an ice cream truck. And then a young girl's voice. "Hi, it's me! Meet me at blue hour. You know where."

The voice loops once more with the same line.

"Hi, it's me! Meet me at blue hour. You know where."

And one more time.

"Meet me at blue hour. You know where."

Does the term blue hour mean anything to you?

The tape ends and I don't notice that I'm crying until I see teardrops fall on the Walkman and realize they must be mine. My head is aching like the beginnings of a migraine.

What is this? I have the strongest feeling that I should know, that somewhere deep inside my mind I do know, but it keeps slipping through my fingers. The girl's voice sounds like Yena, but I don't know what these sounds mean and I don't know why I'm crying. I rewind the tape, let it play again from the start even as my headache grows worse, and I try to remember. I try so hard but nothing comes to mind.

After the third listen, I let the cassette tape reach the end, and I just sit there, numb. I don't know what I'm supposed to feel.

You'll most likely find yourself reading about it online and connecting the dots, Danielle's note said. I pull out the earphones and pick up my phone. I search up: *Danielle Flores, Sori Clinic.*

The first thing that pops up is an article written by

Danielle, posted just an hour ago. But it already has thousands of views, comments, and shares.

The title reads: *I Went Undercover at Sori of Us Clinic and Here's What I Found.*

I first heard of Sori of Us Clinic when I was sixteen. The first of its kind, Sori of Us Clinic—Sori Clinic for short—based in Busan, South Korea, specializes in memory erasing. Formerly the stuff of science fiction, this technology is brought to life by Dr. Mira Bae through a curious method: collecting sounds related to the targeted memory and using mixtape-based technology to erase it.

The sheer impossibility and aesthetic of it alone are enough to pique interest. There's something innately nostalgic about a technology so new mixed with relics of our past, even in its foreignness.

At first, I was as intrigued as any other teenager living in Orange County, California, would be: from afar. But that was before my mother passed away and my father decided that the best way to move on from her death would be to erase her entirely from his memory. In one clean sweep, he removed any reminder of her from our home (save for my siblings and me), flew to South Korea, and had her wiped from his mind. He forgot her smile, forgot the fact that she was a casual chess champion at our local park, forgot the way she looked when she wore her favorite yellow dress. He forgot their whole relationship and the love that came with it, love that would have found a way to carry on but instead got buried in a place that you can no longer visit.

Where does grief go when you erase the person for whom you are grieving? I know where it went for my father—it became caged in his chest like a wild animal unaware of its own captivity—but what about for others? Was erasure a worthwhile endeavor for anyone or did it always end only in more pain? I became obsessed with these questions. So when an opportunity arose to work part-time at Sori Clinic while studying abroad in South Korea, I couldn't pass up the chance to take a look for myself. I applied for the job. I was hired.

Though the work assigned to me was largely administrative, my time at the clinic was illuminating. I crossed paths with protestors who shared stories about family members who had gone through the erasure, only to become addicted to the process. Any time they had any issues, they would simply erase them instead of learning how to deal with them. There were stories of people who would erase their own wrongdoings to relieve themselves of the guilt they carried, people who suffered chronic migraines and nausea afterward, and people who had memories erased that they hadn't even intended to.

"The process is not perfect," Dr. Mira Bae was

quoted as saying in an interview with the *Boston Globe*. But with something as sensitive as memory, should the process not be as close to perfect as possible before being made available to the masses? With the boom of Sori Clinic's success and rapid growth, should there not be more care in the handling of how this life-altering procedure is rolled out? Credit where credit is due, Dr. Bae is certainly a brilliant mind, and a once-in-a-generation talent. In my time working with her, I found her to be a thoughtful boss and the most driven person I've ever met in my life. I do not seek to take away from any of that or to diminish her successes. Rather, I question whether the very field of memory erasure should exist at all.

Within Sori Clinic itself, I had a fellow coworker who had just discovered that her childhood best friend had erased her from his memory. Upon a chance reunion with this friend, she became distraught at the revelation, wrestling with questions of what it means to be so purposefully and irrevocably forgotten. The strangest part? This coworker is the very daughter of Dr. Mira Bae. If Dr. Bae cannot even protect her own family members from the aftermath of this technology, who is truly safe?

To remember someone is to recognize who they were in your life, whether good or bad, big or small. To erase this truth, no matter how painful it might be, is to create holes in your life story that you will inevitably fall into, dragging others in with you. Because the fact of the matter is that those who do the erasing forget that there are people on the other side who still remember; and when you break the chain of remembering together, you cannot be surprised when everybody starts to fall.

17

YENA

I saw the article.

Of course I saw it.

It's the first thing that pops up when you look up Sori Clinic online and everyone at the clinic is talking about it. The celebratory mood in the staff room has been squashed, the sparkling pear juice tucked away. But I don't stick around to respond to Joanne's look of sympathy or stop and chat with Tony when he tries to catch my eye in the hall. No, I get the hell out of there and head straight for Pusan National University.

"Danielle, it's Yena. We have to talk," I say into the phone, leaving my tenth voicemail in the past thirty minutes. "I'm on campus, by the main entrance. I don't know where your dorm is, but you better believe I will knock on every door until I find you and I will be screaming your name in the hallways until you answer. Yes, that is a promise and yes, I will make it extra embarrassing. Call me back."

I hang up, heart pounding in my chest.

I don't understand what I just learned. How could I have

had a piece of my memory erased? It's not the same as what Lucas did. He doesn't even recognize me. But I remember everything about him except for this one thing. I just . . . can't even really say what that one thing is.

I'm freaking out. This is too much. I stumble onto a staircase and sit down, holding my head between my knees before I throw up. The headache from earlier has been coming in ebbs and flows, but I'm not sure if the nausea is another side effect or just a natural response to how shaken I am. Either way, I feel like I'm going to hurl. Students taking summer classes pass me by, books tucked into the crooks of elbows, backpacks slung over shoulders, but I hardly register them. I'm too busy losing my mind.

A shadow falls over me and I look up.

Danielle stands in front of me, hands clasped together. "Hi," she says.

Hi. It's such an ordinary greeting for a day that's anything but, and the audacity of it makes me laugh. It comes out empty and humorless.

She sits next to me, hands still folded, fingers fidgeting over each other. In all my time knowing Danielle, I've never seen her nervous, but that's how she looks now.

I thought about what I would say to her the whole way here, but suddenly all words escape me. I'm just overwhelmed. I don't know where to begin or where to end. "When you said you're a writer . . . ," I finally say.

"I'm a journalist," she says.

"'I Went Undercover at Sori of Us Clinic and Here's What I Found,'" I quote. "Were you planning on writing this article from the moment you got the job?"

"No. I knew from the moment I applied for it."

I think back to all our interactions. Were there any hints? Any signs? If there were, I never caught any of them. She was just doing her job, lying low. I guess that means she's pretty good at the undercover thing.

The betrayal feels like acid in my throat. I get up, start pacing, because I can't sit still with it threatening to choke me.

"That time you first told me about your dad," I say. "I asked you if it's hard to work at Sori Clinic and be reminded of it all the time. And you said your mentor encouraged you, said it could be a great experience for your writing."

"I never lied to you, Yena," Danielle says. "That was all true."

Honestly, I don't know if that makes it better or worse. "So when I was telling you all about Lucas? When I found his mixtape? You were, what, making mental notes to use it as exposure?"

At this, her face falls. She looks down at her hands and then back up at me. There's an apology in her eyes, but no regret. "I wasn't planning on including your story from the start. But Yena, you're Dr. Bae's daughter. That's a personal hook to the story that I just couldn't leave out. I didn't name you—"

"You may as well have!" I cry. "Reporters know who I am. They've already swarmed me once."

Wait. How did the reporters know who I am? That night when they circled me outside Sori Clinic, protestors holding signs around them. They knew my name. They called it out.

"Were you the one that told them?" I ask.

"I didn't tell the reporters who you are," Danielle says quickly. "But . . . I might have mentioned it to some of the protestors I'm friends with. And I don't know who they told." She hangs her head, biting her lip. "I'm sorry if I put you in danger. It never even crossed my mind that that could be an option. All the protests were so peaceful."

It's one whiplash after another. And I haven't even asked about the biggest thing.

"My tape?" I say, voice quiet.

"I noticed the patient name for Tape 202 was blocked on the system so we couldn't see it, and it took me ages to find the tape itself. It was hidden in a section of the Archive that Dr. Bae said she'd taken care of already," Danielle says. "I felt like she was hiding something, so I had a coder friend help me hack it. When I saw your name, I listened to the tape, and I thought you'd want to know. That's the only reason I shared it with you." She hesitates. "Was I wrong about that?"

Was she? I'm not sure yet. I had so many questions about me and Lucas, and now there's this huge piece to add to it. What was the memory? Why did I erase it?

I sit back down on the staircase next to Danielle, hug my knees to my chest. It's all so confusing, but deep down, there's a small part of me that feels almost relieved to know the truth, even if I can't see the whole picture yet. Maybe for some people, knowing this would break them, and even a week ago I'd say that'd be me. But now it feels almost as though it's cracked something open, unearthing something I should have never forgotten in the first place.

"You didn't mention that part in your article," I say. "I bet people would have flocked to a story about Dr. Bae's daughter getting an erasure done herself."

Danielle smiles a little. "That part felt like something that should just be yours."

"Your boundaries are very gray," I say.

She tentatively holds out a hand and places it on my shoulder. I don't move away. "I'm sorry, Yena," she says. "I meant what I said in the note. I never intended to hurt you and betray your trust. But memory erasing isn't right, and I had to speak up about it. It only buries things that shouldn't be and causes pain in the long run."

Knowing the role Sori Clinic played in hurting Danielle's family, can I blame her for feeling this way? For writing what she did? I always knew there were people who were against Mom's work. This isn't the first time protestors have knocked on her door or articles have sprung up speaking out against erasure. But it is the first time it's hit me this hard.

How does Mom deal with it? Living far away from her meant that she wasn't really in my life these past few years, but it also meant that I wasn't really in hers. I have no idea how she navigates all of this on a daily basis. And I have absolutely no clue how she felt about me getting an erasure.

I thought I would never want to talk to her about anything ever again, but I realize I still have things I need to say.

"Listen, Danielle," I say. "I'm pissed that you included me in your article. I feel like that's got to go against some journalism ethics code too, doesn't it? Sharing stories without permission?"

"It was an undercover exposé," Danielle says, but at this, there is a twinge of guilt in her face.

"Okay. Sure. I can't stop you from writing what you want to write, even if it's shitty of you to do it. And even though I hate that you did . . ." I take a deep breath. "I also hate that you were so hurt by Sori Clinic. I can't imagine going through what you did with your parents." It's hard for me to say it when the sting of her betrayal is still so fresh, but when I was reading her article, I found myself not disagreeing with all of it. And I hate that too, how I want to hate her more, but there's a part of me that understands, no matter how begrudgingly.

Danielle blinks at me, at a loss for words. "Thanks," she finally says, her voice quiet. "And I'm really, really sorry."

I nod and stand, walking away. And then I pause, turning back around.

"Lucas is going to see that article, isn't he?" I say. "What did you do with his mixtape?"

She rises to her feet as well. "I sent him a moment of epiphany."

18

LUCAS

Dr. Mira Bae's office is pristine and, frankly, kind of boring.

The walls are white, the desk is glass, and there's not a single plant or piece of artwork to be seen. There is, however, a retro pink clock on the wall that is very out of place but gives a certain charm to the otherwise stock-photo-looking office.

"Lucas Pak," Dr. Bae says when I knock on the door and enter the room. "Welcome. I'm glad we were able to get you a spot in our Memory Recovery Study."

"Me too," I say. My head is still ringing but thankfully it hasn't turned into a full-blown migraine yet. I take a seat across from her as she pulls up the forms I filled out, looking it over.

I haven't seen her since that very first day I walked into Sori Clinic and we ran into each other in the hall. Back then, she was only Dr. Bae, distinguished head of the clinic and leader in the field of memory erasing. Now when I look at her, I also see traces of Yena. They have the same eyes.

"I understand you signed up for your grandfather," she

says. "It said in our email that he should be in attendance for this meeting. Will he be joining us?"

"Actually," I say, "there's been a slight change. This meeting is for me."

She pauses, fingers going still over the forms. "For you? Do you have problems with memory loss as well?"

I pull my mixtape out of my pocket and slide it across the table. "Something like that."

My heart pounds inside my chest. I don't know if this was a good idea. When the time came around to go to the intake appointment I'd booked, I made an impulse decision. I have questions. I need answers. And if I can't convince Harabeoji to take this slot, I'll take it for myself.

Dr. Bae stares at the tape between us, labeled *Patient 201*. Her expression doesn't change, but there's a practiced casualness to her voice when she says, "That looks like one of our tapes. How did you get that?"

"I received it from one of your staff, Danielle Flores. Or former staff, I should say."

At the mention of Danielle's name, Dr. Bae sighs, pinching the bridge of her nose. I assume she saw the article. I'd be surprised if she hadn't. It's blown up even more since it was first posted, trending all over social media. There are a thousand different opinions in the online conversation, each one louder than the last.

A friend of mine had the erasure and I've truly never seen him more at peace with himself, one commenter wrote.

Some people need a little bit of help letting go, especially when it comes to traumatic events, and there is nothing wrong with that.

How would you know how he really feels? another commenter replied. *Even if he's still unhappy, how can he talk about it now if he doesn't know why?*

There are people agreeing with Danielle and people defending Dr. Bae and people contributing nothing to the conversation but extra noise. I'm not sure what I think myself. But from the beginning, it wasn't the process of forgetting that I was most interested in. It was the possibility of remembering.

"I'd like to try and recover the memories on this tape," I say. "All the sounds are already here, recorded and ready to go. Can we do that?"

At first, Dr. Bae doesn't speak. She turns the tape over in her hands and then lays it flat on the table again. "Answer a few questions for me first, Lucas," she says. "Do you know what it is you're trying to recover? Do you have any idea what you might remember if you open this door?"

The sounds of the tape come back to me, of Yena's voice and blue hour and the strange things that Harabeoji has said, the even stranger things I've been seeing and hearing inside my own mind.

"I don't have an exact idea," I say slowly. "But I think it's something important. Something I shouldn't have forgotten."

"You erased it for a reason," she points out.

"Reasons can change, can't they?"

She watches me carefully. "I need to tell you the full risk of trying to restore these memories. There's a chance it won't be possible. You could remember, but you could also come out of it the same as you began. And, worst-case scenario, you may even lose a few related memories in the attempt. This is something we tell all our participants in the study, and they come much more prepared than you do today with a companion to assist them and give us a sense of what we're trying to recover in the first place. If you are asking for my professional opinion, I would advise against it."

I swallow hard. When I was thinking of the study as a hypothetical for Harabeoji, any risk seemed worthwhile if it could potentially make things better. But sitting across from Dr. Bae and hearing it laid out so plainly as a real possibility, I can't help but feel nervous. I could come out of this with a few less memories than when I started. And if what I'm thinking is correct and the sounds on the mixtape are related to Yena, then the memories I've made with her this summer are the most susceptible to disappearing if the process goes wrong.

I think of her, literally crashing into my life when she ran into me outside the clinic. Her eyes, her voice, the twist of her hair as she clips it into place. I think of the way she looked when she was surrounded by reporters, the relief in her laugh when we were far away and safe, eating skewers in a tent, recording the sound of book pages flying beneath her fingers. I might forget the warmth of her in my arms, of her hands on my face, telling me to breathe.

I don't want to forget.

I'm terrified that I will. That I already have.

"Can I ask you something first?" I ask.

"You can ask me anything."

"Have you had any successful attempts in your study so far to recover memories lost to illness or a condition in the brain?"

"No."

"What about preemptively protecting memories so they don't ever get lost to these causes?"

"We don't have enough data yet to say one way or the other. Time is a factor."

"Okay. Last question. Have you ever recovered a memory that was lost to erasure?"

At this, a small smile makes her lips quirk up. "We have had one successful procedure so far that fits that description, yes. We were able to fully recover a memory that we originally erased. It's a promising step forward in exploring how far memory restoration can go."

I take a deep breath. "My case would fit that description as well, would it not?"

She considers this. "It would technically, yes," she says slowly. "Though I should tell you that in this successful case, we had more to work with than you do right now.

The patient, with the help of their assisting family member, was able to bring in recordings of things they still currently remembered that were related to the memory they lost. Weaving the sounds of the forgotten memory with more recent non-forgotten ones was what made it enough to bring it back. But you only have the sounds of what you've already lost. I can't guarantee that'll work the same way."

"Related recent memories that I still remember," I say, turning the implication of this over in my mind. I reach into my pocket and pull out the recording device that I've been carrying with me all summer, placing it on the table. "Will this do?"

Dr. Bae raises her eyebrows. "Well, at this point I'm simply curious how much more of our property you have on you."

"I may not know exactly what I'm trying to remember, but I know it has something to do with this girl," I say. "There are sounds here from all the things we did together this summer. And I remember everything about that."

I leave out Yena's name, but I'm certain Dr. Bae must know what I'm talking about and that she and I have met before. I don't go into specifics though. She's the best in this business. If I want to remember, I need her help, and I don't want to broach the topic of a potential conflict of interest.

"I hear you about the risk," I say. "But as a participant in the Memory Recovery Study, I'm willing to take that risk. I think what's on the other end is worthwhile enough to try everything I can to get it back."

Saying it out loud, I realize how much I believe it. I believed it for Harabeoji and I believe it for me, only now I get that I can't force this kind of decision onto anyone else no matter how honest my intentions might be. I can't control other people, or really much of anything in life. I can only make my own choices.

For a long, extended moment of silence, I think Dr. Bae is going to say no. But then she gives me a decisive nod, picking up both the mixtape and the recording device from the table. "All right," she says. "Let's proceed."

We walk down the hall toward the procedure room and with every step, my heart beats louder and louder in my ears. Before we left Dr. Bae's office, she gave me the choice to go through the recovery process today or book an appointment for a later date.

"I understand that you might not be mentally prepared to do this immediately, no matter what decision you've arrived at," she said. "That's perfectly fine. If you choose to do it today, we do have an open window right now. You would arrange to have someone pick you up after the procedure, or if you'd prefer, we have staff that can accompany you home. The entire process can range from one to three hours, depending on the amount of memory material we're working with. If you decide to do it at a later date, our earliest opening would be next week, and we can stop for today."

"Today," I said. "I'll do it today." By tomorrow, I won't even be in Korea anymore.

"Would you like to call anyone to arrange for pick up?"

I imagined telling Harabeoji or Samchon what I'm about to do. How would I even begin to explain this?

"No," I said. "I'll take the option to have staff accompany me. Though, will I really need it?"

"You'll be given anesthesia during the procedure, so we do want to make sure you're looked after. Though you can take your time here in one of our recovery rooms until you're ready to go. Usually with erasures, we want patients to wake up at home so they don't know they were ever at Sori Clinic, but of course this is quite different."

So I signed the waivers and followed her out of her office. As nervous as I am walking down this hallway, I don't back away from my decision. I want to do this. I have to do this.

She stops outside a door and opens it. "After you."

I step inside. I'm not sure what I'm expecting to see, but it looks like a cross between a dentist's office and recording booth. There's a chair that leans all the way back, presumably for the patient to sit in, with a pair of strange headphones hanging on a stand next to it. They look almost like regular wireless headphones, but with various purple wires springing from the body like spider legs. The recording booth area looks more complex, with a wall of cassette tape machines and multiple screens and dial boards, all alight in different colors.

Dr. Bae introduces her assistant Tony, who is already sitting in the booth and will be helping with the procedure. He comes over to shake my hand. His hand is warm and reassuring. Mine is starting to sweat profusely.

Dr. Bae explains how everything is going to work, but I'm beginning to get so nervous that I'm only half paying attention. Something about how I'll be wearing these special headphones—she explains how each of the wires will be attached to my head and feeding information to the screens that she'll be monitoring the whole time—and I'll be asleep for most of it. "You won't feel a thing," she says.

"Uh-huh," I say.

Tony guides me into the chair, leaning it back, and begins to prepare the anesthesia. "It won't kick in immediately," he says. "You'll find yourself dozing off to the sounds of the tape. Any questions before we continue?"

So many questions but none that he can answer right now. I shake my head.

Tony administers the anesthesia, fastens the headphones over my ears, attaches the wires, and disappears into the recording booth part of the room with Dr. Bae. At first, I hear nothing. And then I hear wind chimes.

Suddenly, I panic. What if this does go wrong? What if I forget Yena?

A film reel. Her laugh. A bustling fish market.

I don't want to lose her. I don't want to forget her.

The Beach Train. A lawn mower.

No. I *won't* forget her.

Street food oil and the sound of waves.

I won't forget.

And then, just as Yena's voice begins to ebb into my consciousness, I hear nothing at all.

SOUND

THE WATER
14 YEARS OLD

They wanted to race.

The girl had challenged the boy to it weeks ago as soon as they knew they were going to the lake with his family. She said that the winner could ask the loser to tell any truth or do any dare. The boy accepted. He already knew what he would ask her if he won.

It was a beautiful day at the lake. The boy's parents had the day off work and brought a grill. His grandfather barbecued long strips of sizzling pork belly and they ate it wrapped in lettuce with spoonfuls of rice.

"It was nice of your parents to invite me," the girl said as they walked to the shore to meet me. "I always thought they didn't like me very much."

"They like you," the boy said, but it sounded unconvincing.

She frowned.

"And Harabeoji loves you," he said. That sounded more true and it made her smile. But there was something in the word *love* that also made her cheeks turn pink.

The boy must have noticed too because he cleared his throat awkwardly and said, "About yesterday at the ice cream truck—"

She shielded her eyes from the sun, interrupting. "Where should we race to? The floating dock and back?"

He hesitated but let her change the subject. "Sounds good. Should we make it more interesting and say best out of three?"

"Fine." She stuck out her hand for him to shake. "Best out of three."

The weather was warm, but I was cold, and neither of them were expecting it as they ran into the lake. The girl screeched. "It's supposed to be summer!"

"Sorry, what did you say? I'm too busy beating you," he said over his shoulder, diving in to swim.

They raced, to the floating dock and back to the shore. First he won, and then she did, and then she won again.

"Victory is mine!" she exclaimed, flopping down onto the sand and throwing peace signs into the air.

"Wait wait wait," the boy said. "Let's do best out of five. I got held up by that stuck kayak in the last round."

"Seriously?"

"Seriously. Unless . . . you're tired?"

She sat up abruptly. "No way. I could swim forever." She paused. "But snack break first?"

They took a break, eating chips and Oreos, lazing in the sun, tossing a volleyball back and forth with his grandfather.

And then before they knew it, the sun began to set, and his parents started packing up their things.

"Wait! We still have to finish our race," the boy said.

"Huh? You're going swimming again?" his father said.

"We lost track of time. We have to finish." He was already running back toward me, the girl at his heels.

"We'll be right back!" she called over her shoulder.

With the sun slowly sinking, I was even colder now, but that didn't deter them. They leapt into the lake, shrieking and shivering, and swam. This time, the boy won.

"It's tied," he said. "One last race for everything."

"We should make it more interesting, then," the girl said. "We swim out even farther." She squinted, pointing past the floating dock. "You see that buoy?"

"All the way out there? That's pretty far."

"Scared?"

He grinned. "No way. Ready? Three, two, one . . . go!"

They were good swimmers, both of them. They could feel the rhythm of my pulse and follow it, moving closer and closer toward the buoy. The sky was indigo now, dark enough that if you looked from the shore, you might not even see the two kids swimming. You might not see one of them suddenly falter, a cramp in his leg, and you certainly wouldn't hear him open his mouth and begin to say, "Hey, wait—" because before he could get the words out, a wave rolled over his head, submerging his voice.

I rushed into his ears and he was stunned by how loud

I can be, how deafening. Perhaps it was the boat that was passing by, making the waves rougher than they were a minute ago, or the fact that there was no more sunlight to guide his way, but the boy was struggling. He thrashed against me, trying to find his way to the surface, but his leg was holding him back, pulling him down. His own panic was working against him, disorienting his sense of direction.

No. He wanted to win. He had to win. He already had his truth and dare picked out.

If she chose truth, he'd ask her, *How would you feel if I told you that I loved you too?*

If she chose dare, he'd say, *Can I kiss you?*

Even though the rules said the loser had to oblige, he wouldn't make her. He just knew that today was the day he had to tell her how he felt. That he loved her. That he wanted to kiss her.

Instead, he was going to die.

He thought he could hear her voice yelling his name. Two voices yelling his name. And then, just when it felt like his lungs were going to burst, a pair of arms hooked around him, dragging him to the surface.

He gasped for air. His grandfather held him tight, swimming to the floating dock. "You're okay," he said. "You're okay."

The boy collapsed on the dock, where the girl ran to him, throwing her arms around his neck, her shoulders heaving with sobs. "Oh my god. Oh my god. I was so scared."

"I'm okay," he croaked. His grandfather climbed onto the dock next to him, patting his back. On the shore, he saw his parents, submerged halfway themselves as if about to dive in, following after his grandfather to save him. He gave them a half-hearted wave to show that he was fine.

They didn't look too happy.

After that, I was the lullaby that met him in his dreams. He couldn't seem to shake me. Sometimes he would break free to the surface and sometimes he would sink. But always he would think of her. Even after the details of her faded and he could no longer place the feeling into words, he carried it in his sleep—the loss of never having told her that he loved her.

19

YENA

Google Calendar Invite:

Stardust Roller Rink, Mom and Yena, 7:00 p.m.

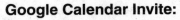

I almost don't accept the invitation, but in the end, I do. I know I need to talk to her. I've spent the whole day wrestling with how I feel about everything that's come to light and I realize I won't fully know until I see her, until I finally have all the pieces that I'm missing.

When I arrive at Stardust, she's already there, sitting under the pink lights, lacing up her roller skates. She looks up and spots me. Even though she's right across the room, I feel like the distance between us is greater than the ocean. I stand, unmoving, staring at her.

She gets up first, rolling over to me and holding out a second pair of roller skates. "Want to go on the rink?" she asks.

I'm confused. Did she invite me here to skate together? "I've never done it before," I say.

"I'll show you how. Come on."

My confusion grows but so does my curiosity. I cautiously take the roller skates and put them on, following her onto the rink.

We glide under the disco ball—or she glides. I awkwardly stumble along as she teaches me how to move forward, how to turn, how to stop. Watching her skate from afar that first time, I could tell she was a natural. But actually being on the rink with her myself, I see how good she really is.

"How long have you been coming here?" I ask.

"For ages. I first found it when I was on exchange here in my undergrad," she says. "That was the time I really fell in love with Busan."

I try to picture Mom as a university student coming here to roller-skate with her friends, dancing on wheels, singing along to the K-pop songs playing over the speakers like the people around us are doing now. A week ago, I would have never been able to imagine it. But having seen her here already, looking so in her element, it's not hard to believe anymore.

"This place was like a refuge for me when I was going through tough times," she says. I get the hang of moving forward and we slowly do a lap around the rink. "Whenever I would put on these roller skates, I would forget about everything that was causing me stress. School. Friend drama. It was the first place I came when I got the news that my mom had passed away."

"You've never talked about her much," I say. The only

thing Mom has ever told me about my grandma is that she died before I was born.

"We weren't very close," Mom says. "She was addicted to gambling and only called me to borrow money until I cut her off. I was just a student and I had a lot of resentment toward her. But still, when she was gone, I came here to skate and I cried for hours on the rink."

"Oh . . ." My heart feels heavy at her story and I let out a deep sigh. If she was in undergrad, she would have only been a few years older than me when that happened.

"It was while I was here, actually, that I had the idea of starting Sori Clinic," Mom says.

"Really?" I never knew that. Come to think of it, I don't know too many details about Mom's history of becoming Dr. Bae. I never had much of a chance to ask.

"I was already on track to pursue neuroscience with a specialty in memory studies. And I thought, what if I could bottle this feeling of forgetting and offer it to people who are struggling, who need extra help beyond what roller skating or anything else in the world can offer them? What if I could give a fresh start to people who feel like they're at a dead end?"

She skates backward to face me, and I can imagine her clearer than ever, young and brilliant and ambitiously dreaming of a future that didn't yet exist.

"Has it been what you thought it would be?" I ask.

She considers this, thoughtful. "In some ways, it's been everything I could have hoped for. There were a lot of people who were betting on my failure and still are. That number is probably only growing by the day, but despite all the challenges, I've had my fair share of wins. Many people have found what they needed through Sori Clinic, and I have a wonderful, smart, capable team that I have the privilege of leading." She gives me a wry smile. "That said, I'd be lying if I said I never thought about quitting. I always knew it was a controversial field to get into, but I didn't realize how much of my energy would be directed at navigating that. And of course, I constantly feel like I'm either failing or right on the brink of it."

"You? Failing?" I say, not even trying to mask my surprise. "Please, Mom. You're the most successful person I know. And what about all those wins you mentioned?"

"It's always a relief when things work out, but then I go right back to holding my breath like I'm waiting for the other shoe to drop," she says honestly. "I know what strengths I'm capable of, but more than anyone else, I also know what my fallibilities are and how loudly some people root for my downfall."

We start on our second lap around the rink and I can't help but wonder what this summer would have been like if I had known this earlier, that Mom is also someone who feels unsure about herself sometimes. Would I have opened up to her about Lucas sooner? Been less scared to bring up hard things with her? Mom and I have never had a perfect relationship, but I could pretend for a long time that it was fine enough. How different would things have been if we both pretended a little less?

"Are you talking about Danielle's article?" I ask, referring to her downfall comment.

"Yeah. And the many other articles and news reports and personal phone calls I receive saying as much. Though Danielle is the only one who brought my daughter into the conversation." She looks at me seriously, examining my face. "Are you okay?"

The concern and care in her voice catches me off guard. When was the last time she asked me something like that? I look away for a few seconds, concentrating only on my roller skates as I try to gather my words. "I think I'm okay," I say. "I talked to Danielle today and even though I'm so, so angry with her at what she did, I can't blame her completely. Sori Clinic really messed with her life."

Mom nods somberly. "I know."

"There's something else though that Danielle and I talked about," I say. My throat feels suddenly dry, but I force myself to keep going. "Something I wanted to ask you about."

"Is it about your mixtape?" she asks.

My mouth drops open. "How did you know?"

"I noticed that someone hacked our system to look at your file in the online database," she says. "And when I found your tape missing from the Archive, I figured either you had found it or Danielle had and it was only a matter of time before she'd show you."

I gape at her. I don't know what to say. "How long have you known this for?"

"Not very long at all. Though it has been a long, long time that I've been wanting to talk to you about this. I never knew how or if I should, but with everything that's happened this summer, I think now is the time." She looks nervous now. "Four years ago, Lucas wasn't the only one who got his memory erased. You did too."

My eyes widen. I'm so stunned to hear it out loud from her own lips that I nearly lose my balance and fall right over. She reaches over and takes my arm, steadying me. I don't let go of her as we keep moving, bracing myself for what she's about to tell me.

"You went to the lake with Lucas and his family one day, and you challenged him to a race," she says. "You two were swimming. It was getting dark, and you swam out too far. When you turned around, you didn't see Lucas anymore. You said you panicked and tried to find him, but you couldn't. You called for help and Lucas's grandfather came running.

"Luckily, he was a good swimmer and he saved Lucas

just in time. Lucas was okay. But then he started having nightmares, panic attacks. You said his parents didn't want him to see you anymore, that you felt like they blamed you. So you called me. You asked if I could erase the incident from both of your minds. Even then, you were scared of losing him. You didn't want things to change."

I cling tighter to Mom's arm as she tells the story. My story. I don't remember the lake day or calling Mom, asking her to erase our memories, but there's a feeling I have hearing her words, the same feeling I had when I was talking to Danielle earlier today. Like there's something cracking open inside me. There's also that headache again, ebbing and flowing, growing a little stronger with Mom's words.

"You said yes," I say quietly. "You did the erasure."

"You were both minors and needed parent permission," she says. "I was reluctant, but Lucas's parents agreed so I did too. You all flew out to Korea for it, had your tapes all ready for the procedure. Your dad just thought it was a regular visit. We knew he wouldn't approve of the erasure. I told him not to bring up what happened at the lake with you in the future with the excuse that you didn't ever want to talk about it again."

"I remember that trip," I say. "Kind of."

I know I went to Korea to visit Mom for a week, but I can't recall much of what we did. I guess this explains why.

"When Lucas's family arrived, I noticed their tape seemed

to contain more memories than the lake incident. When I asked them if they'd like me to revise it, they said no." At this, she looks away from me, concentrating straight ahead on the rink. "His parents asked me to erase you entirely from his mind. They said they had already been planning on moving away before this happened, but Lucas didn't want to leave you behind. He was struggling badly with that as well as the trauma of nearly drowning. They wanted to give him a fresh start in a new city and were worried you would hold him back. He didn't know what they were asking."

When she looks back at me again, there are tears in her eyes. We stop skating, standing under the disco ball. "When I said I feel like a failure, I don't just mean in my work. I mean as a mom too. I know there are so many ways I've let you down, but of all of them, the one that's haunted me the most is not taking your side that day. A part of me felt like it was my fault that the lake incident had happened in the first place, that me moving away made you more reckless, more irresponsible. I was trying to make things right by agreeing to their request, but I should have been thinking about you. I'm sorry."

So there it is. All the questions I had, all the answers I was looking for. I'm silent, my own eyes pricking with tears. How ironic that the idea to get an erasure was mine in the first place, that my fear of losing another person I loved was the thing that made it happen.

No, I tell myself. That's not right. I didn't make all this happen. I was a kid. I was a scared kid who reacted, and other people made decisions that would change both my life and Lucas's without telling us. All this time I've been worried that it was my fault he erased me, wondering what I could have possibly done wrong to warrant something so final, so harsh. I thought I was the problem because I'm always the problem. But I didn't choose this. Neither of us did.

"You're right, Mom," I say, the tears slipping loose and falling down my cheeks. "You should have taken my side."

She takes my hands in hers and I let her, and then she rolls me closer and wraps her arms around my shoulders. I can feel her crying too, her whole body shaking, or maybe it's me, maybe it's both of us. We keep crying like that as people skate around us, crying for the mistakes that were made, the time that was lost, the words that weren't said for far too long. I wonder what all the other people on the rink think of us and I realize I don't care.

"What now?" I ask when we finally let each other go. Her face is streaked with tears and I can probably guess that I don't look much different. I wipe my eyes with the back of my hand.

She leads me off the rink and says, "Well, Danielle's article did make me think. About how communal memories are and how one person forgetting can cause a fracture in the chain of shared experiences." She sits me down on a bench, gesturing for me to untie my roller skates. "I wanted you both to have the same information again to start repairing the chain."

"Both?" I ask, confused.

She passes me my shoes. "You should get going. There's someone waiting for you at Sori Clinic."

For a long time, I wondered what the point of anything is when nothing lasts forever. Not even close to forever. The things you cherish most in the world can vanish in the blink of an eye, no matter how tightly you hold on, no matter how hard you try to make sure it stays the same.

I turn the corner toward Sori Clinic, using Mom's key to enter through the back door to avoid the big group that's gathered outside the building again, a mix of protestors and reporters no doubt responding to Danielle's article. I definitely don't want to deal with that right now. I slip into the building unnoticed, making my way up to the office.

Maybe forever doesn't exist. But then there are moments like this. Moments like when I walk into the recovery room where Lucas is sitting up in bed, staring out the window at the setting sun, the sky alight in blue and pink and orange. The sun and the moon share space for the briefest of moments, and Lucas turns to look at me with pure recognition in his eyes, like he's been waiting a lifetime to remember me. He stands and then he's walking across the room, and I realize I want to hold on to this, every single detail of it. Not to try to make it last forever but because I know it won't, and if that's not worth treasuring, I don't know what is.

Lucas is right in front of me now. "Hi," he says, his voice hoarse. He's the same but different. The Lucas I've always known, the Lucas I got to know this summer.

"Hi," I say.

He points to the sky outside the window. "It's blue hour. When the sky is most in love with itself."

And I wrap my arms around his neck and I kiss him. I kiss him like I always wanted to, with everything I am, with everything that makes my heart full, and he kisses me back the same, hands around my waist, tangled in my hair. I pull back to touch his cheek, to remind myself that this is real.

"I missed you," I say.

"Same," he says, pressing his forehead against mine.

I laugh. "Is that all?"

He presses a palm against my face, looks me in the eye. "I missed you. And I love you. I wanted to say that for so long. I love you. I love you. I'm sorry I forgot."

A lump rises in my throat. I lean in, hold him tight, as tight as I can. "Same," I say.

We stand there as the sky grows dark, clinging to each

other under the fading light. Blue hour. When the rest of the city is slowing down, getting ready to sleep, he's here running to me and I'm here, waiting for him. And somehow, against all odds, we've found ourselves home again.

20

LUCAS

I hold the eggs gently in one hand, cracking them directly into the stone pot. Harabeoji hums as I whisk them, sitting at the table.

"It's hot today," he says.

"Should I make the air con stronger?"

"I don't want to be too cold."

"Here." I run into his room and grab a handheld fan, holding it out to him. "You can fan yourself with this. Your favorite fan."

"Favorite fan. I have a favorite fan?" he chuckles.

I smile and finish preparing the gyeran jjim.

It's been almost a week since I recovered the memories on my mixtape. It was strange and jarring at first, being reminded of things that had been blocked out of my mind for so long. It was like flinging the curtains open after being in the dark for years and learning to see in the sunlight again. The migraines were bad those first few days. Dr. Bae prescribed me some medicine to help with that, and things have slowly been getting better.

Still, it's odd. My brain feels sensitive, if that's even possible. Every time I've seen Yena since, I find myself going through old memories, asking, *Did this really happen? Or am I imagining it?* I feel like I can't totally trust my own mind yet.

It wasn't easy telling everyone what happened either. As anti-memory-tampering as he is, Harabeoji was understanding about my decision and glad that everything went well. Though in the days that followed, I'm not sure he remembered our conversation or the fact that I had ever forgotten Yena at all. Any time I brought her up, he'd speak like he did that time in Damyang Forest, like we've been friends this whole time.

Samchon, of course, was shocked and needed a lot of filling in, but he was supportive in his own way. I wasn't ready to talk to my parents yet so he did it for me, telling them that I wouldn't be coming back on the rescheduled flight and that I need some time to myself. When I asked him how they took it, he paused for a long time and said, "I think they have a lot to think about themselves."

Unfortunately, I can't avoid them forever and we have a video call scheduled today (a request relayed from Umma through Samchon to me). Almost exactly on time, my phone rings with an incoming call. I hesitate picking up, but in the end, I do, stepping into Harabeoji's room and closing the door behind me for privacy.

Umma and Appa appear on the screen, sitting side by

side. Umma looks worried and cautious, her eyes puffy as if she's been crying. Appa is more stoic and somber, his arms folded across his chest.

"Hi, Lucas," Umma says tentatively. "Did you eat yet?"

"Just about to." My voice comes out flat and cold. Yena told me the whole story about how and why we got our memories erased, and Dr. Bae had me into her office shortly afterward to personally apologize for how it all happened. I know Yena is working through her own trust issues with her mom after discovering everything, but I don't know how to even begin doing the same with my parents. I feel sick every time I think about what they did. I don't know if I'll ever be able to look at them the same again.

"How's Harabeoji?" Umma asks.

"He's fine."

An awkward silence falls between us.

"Listen, Lucas," Appa says, leaning forward so I can only see half his face on the screen. "Your mom and I called to explain ourselves. And to tell you that we're sorry."

I don't say anything, but I don't hang up on them either.

"Growing up, you and Yena were so close," Umma says. "Sometimes we worried that your friendship was too intense for how young you were. She had a lot of influence over you, and we weren't always sure how good that influence was. And then we made the decision to move to Edmonton and you were so upset. You said you wouldn't go, that we'd have to leave you behind because you didn't want to say goodbye to her. You barely talked to us anymore.

"And then after what happened at the lake, you became even more withdrawn. You weren't eating, you were having nightmares; you were so anxious. We hated seeing you like that. So when the chance came for us to make it better and give you a fresh start, we took it." She hesitates. "Or at least, we thought we could make it better."

"By messing with my head and secretly erasing my memory?" I say, my voice rising with disbelief and anger.

"You were just a kid," Appa says. "We thought we were doing what was best for you and for our family."

"I was fourteen. You could have asked me what I wanted."

"You're right," Umma says, shaking her head. "We could have. We should have."

I can feel a headache coming on, something I've noticed happening more often lately when I feel my stress rising. If I don't manage it in time, it can get really awful. "Hold on," I say, turning the camera off and putting my phone down on Harabeoji's desk. I head back to the kitchen to get a glass of water and calm down before it gets worse.

As I pour myself a glass, I see Harabeoji out of the corner of my eye, opening and closing the handheld fan. He tests it out, fanning himself, the light breeze blowing back wisps of his hair. I pause.

Just a couple of weeks ago, didn't I think that I knew what was best for Harabeoji? That I was in the right and he was the one who didn't understand the situation? How convinced was I that if he could just see what I saw, he'd come around to what a good thing the Memory Recovery Study could be?

But that's different from this. Recovering and taking preventive measures to help his Alzheimer's isn't the same as erasing someone's memories behind their back. Still, I can't help but hesitate. There was a risk that Harabeoji would have had some of his memories erased in the process and I still thought it was worth it even though I knew he was against it. It might not be the exact same situation, but it's enough to give me pause.

I know how it feels to want to go to any lengths to make things better for someone you love, even if it's something they would never agree with.

I finish my water and go back into Harabeoji's room, picking up my phone and turning the camera on again.

"Thanks for apologizing," I say to my parents. "I don't know if I can forgive you yet, or ever, but I hear what you're saying. We'll talk more when I'm back."

Umma and Appa exchange glances and, coming to the conclusion that this is the best they're going to get for now, Appa gives me a small nod. "Okay. We'll see you when you're back at the end of August."

I can't help but ask, "Is the restaurant going to be okay?"

It was hard not to feel guilty about leaving the restaurant in a tough situation by choosing to stay in Korea, but I had to remind myself that it's okay for me to take the space I need. As much as I care about the restaurant, I have to put my own well-being first.

"We'll manage," Umma says. "Your dad and I actually decided to take your advice and close the restaurant for a few days to rest. We realized we were running ourselves and all our staff into the ground and that's no good for the restaurant either. So hopefully a break will help us reset." She pauses. "And maybe when you're back, we can talk about you working in the kitchen? I think I could really use your help in there."

Maybe it's just a peace offering born out of guilt, but my heart lifts a bit hearing that. And as mad as I am at them, I do feel glad to hear about their plans to rest. "Okay," I say. "And good for you for taking a break. I'll talk to you later, then."

"Lucas?" Umma says.

"Yeah?"

"I heard the weather there is extra humid. It's jangma season there. Don't forget to carry around an umbrella so you don't get caught in the rain."

"Okay, Umma. Bye."

We hang up. I stand still for a moment, taking a deep breath. Inhale. Exhale. It's going to be tough moving forward with them, but I survived the first conversation and that's something. So for now, I tuck them into the back of my mind and head back to the kitchen for lunch.

I finish cooking the eggs I prepared earlier on the stove

and set the table: two bowls of purple rice, soy-sauce-braised eggs and meat, cucumber kimchi, and of course, the gyeran jjim, perfectly steamed and extra fluffy. Just the way Harabeoji taught me how to make it.

"This looks great, Taehoon," Harabeoji says.

"It's Lucas, Harabeoji," I say.

He smiles at me and there's a pang in my heart. I don't know if I'll ever get used to the way his memories keep fading, but maybe it's okay to be sad about something without trying to control it. Maybe it's okay just to grieve what something is.

Harabeoji eats a spoonful of gyeran jjim, his eyes growing wide. "This is delicious!"

"Yeah?" I grin, sitting down next to him and reaching for my own spoon. "Maybe I'll teach you how to make it one day."

21

YENA

It's a hot and sticky humid day and Lucas has asked me to meet him at Cheongsapo, so I do. I wait for him under the awning of a convenience store, watching fishermen across the street sitting by the water, casting their lines into the sea.

"You're early," a voice behind me says.

I turn to see Lucas standing there, smiling. He kisses me on the cheek, and I smile back, so big my face hurts.

"Well, I am eighteen today after all," I say. "New me, new leaf, and so on."

"Is that how the saying goes?" he laughs. He takes my hand and starts walking, our arms swinging in time with each other. "Happy birthday, by the way. What did you get up to this morning?"

"I went for a run at Taejongdae." It's a habit I've been sticking to ever since I went with Danielle. Nobody is more surprised than me, but I've actually been enjoying going once a week. Sometimes I see Danielle and we'll run together without saying much. Even though it's still strange between us and we never acknowledge each other with more than a head nod, I can tell she keeps her pace a little slower when I'm with her so I can keep up.

"Are you going to take me sometime?" Lucas asks.

"Hmm, I don't know. I'm pretty fast now. Like, basically athlete level. Not sure if you'd be able to keep up."

He grins. "I'll have to start training then. But hey, look. We're here."

We arrive at the station where we recorded the Beach Train all those weeks ago. Lucas leads me to the top floor of the station, where he pulls out two tickets for the Sky Capsule.

"You're kidding!" I say. "You made reservations?"

"Of course. It's your birthday."

I link my arm through his, touched. "Are you sure you didn't book it because you were disappointed we couldn't ride it together last time?"

"Yes, actually, you're right. It's a birthday gift to me. After this, we'll go watch a movie."

"Sounds like the perfect gift."

"For you or for me?" he teases.

"Hmm." I pretend to think. "For both of us."

We wait in line and board a yellow capsule. I peer out the window as it starts moving slowly along the railway, taking photos with my phone. "I think I can see Sori Clinic from here."

"Really?"

"I mean, hard to say. Most of these office buildings look the same."

There's been a lot of restructuring going on at Sori these days. While they still offer memory erasing as their main service, Dr. Bae is shifting more of her focus to the recovery study, putting more of her time and resources into building up her knowledge there. She's also promoted Joanne to head up the new Post-Erasure Program, open to family and friends of people who have received erasures and are struggling with the impact of the change in their lives. Despite the new schedule, Joanne still finds time to organize the monthly team dinners. I'll be going to my first one this week.

Mom is busier than ever, but somehow, she's trying to find time to have a meal with me twice a week. I get Google Calendar invites for it every Monday.

"Can I ask you something I've always been curious about?" I asked her the last time we had breakfast.

"Sure."

"The pink clock in the apartment. The only piece of decoration you have in the whole place. It looks suspiciously like the one at Stardust Roller Rink."

"Is that a question?"

I raised my eyebrows at her.

She sighed. "Okay. Fine. I'm not the best at interior design. I don't have the time or the eye. But when I think of a place that feels like home, I think of Stardust. So I stole a couple clocks from their wall."

"Stole?" I shrieked, unable to stop the smile in my voice.

"Clocks? Plural? Dr. Bae! I'm shocked at you."

"I know, I know, I should have just asked," she said, face going red. "But I didn't want to seem silly. And they have so many! I should confess one day, huh?"

"I'll go with you," I said. "I want to be there when they take your mug shot."

There are still a lot of years and trust lost between us that we're trying to bridge, but I'm hopeful. I know she's trying and I am too.

"So I've been thinking," Lucas says. I turn away from the window to look at him. He seems nervous. "I know we still have a couple weeks left in Busan, but after that we'll be going back home, right? Me to Edmonton, you to Vancouver."

"That's right," I say.

As tough as things have been with Lucas and his parents lately, I know he still wants to go back to the family restaurant and help keep Lim's Kitchen thriving, with visits to see Harabeoji in Busan as often as he can. And even though I'm still not sure what I want to do next, I feel excited to go back and figure it out, something I never thought I'd feel about my future. Dad is pretty excited about seeing me again too, especially after I filled him in on everything that's happened. He's already cleared his entire calendar for the week I get back so we can have some proper one-on-one catch-up time. Though I did ask him to schedule an ice cream date with me, him, and his girlfriend, Alice.

"Well, I was wondering . . ." Lucas looks up at the ceiling of the capsule and then back at me. "Do you still not do long distance?"

My heart flutters, but I manage to keep my face deadpan. "That depends. Are we talking long-distance friendship or long-distance more than friendship?"

He grins, moving closer to me in the capsule. His face is so close I can count the freckles on his cheeks. "What do you think?"

He leans in and lightly presses his lips against mine, and I'm certain he can feel the smile on my lips as I kiss him back. I'll never get used to this, how good it feels, how *right*.

Someone knocks on the window of our capsule and we break apart, startled. We've arrived at Haeundae Station and the staff member standing on the platform is rolling his eyes, opening the door.

"Thank you for riding the Sky Capsule," he says. "Now get out, please."

We quickly slide out of the capsule and hurry off the platform. As soon as we leave the station, we look at each other and burst out laughing.

Suddenly, a raindrop falls on my nose. And then another, and another, until the whole sky has erupted with rain.

"Monsoon season!" Lucas exclaims, trying to cover our heads with his hands. "I left my umbrella at home."

"Me too," I say. "Come on!"

I grab his hand and we run, laughing, trying to beat the

rain, eighteen and just eighteen, on the brink of unstoppable. If I were to capture us in a mixtape, just as we are right now, it would sound something like this, like the summer monsoon, like his footsteps running next to mine. And it would be the most beautiful thing I've ever heard.

Acknowledgments

I wrote this book. And then I wrote it again from scratch, keeping only the character names, the general premise, and one sentence from the original draft. It took me a long time to figure out Yena and Lucas's story, but I am incredibly proud of where we landed, and I have many people to thank for helping me get here.

To my editor, Jennifer Ung—I always say my books wouldn't be what they are without you, but I feel like this one really took that sentiment to the next level. Thank you for being the compass that led me to the heart of this story when I was feeling so lost in it.

Thank you to Linda Epstein, my agent and champion, for your evergreen support. Thank you also to my foreign rights agent, Taryn Fagerness, for all your enthusiasm in sharing my stories around the world.

I truly feel like the luckiest person to have my name on such a beautiful cover, which is wholly thanks to David Curtis. I love every single thoughtful and creative detail. It is the perfect shade of blue.

Speaking of making this book beautiful, thank you to my copyeditor, Jessica White, my proofreader, Christine

Vahaly, and my production editor, Erin DeSalvatore, without whom this book would be much more of a tangled mess than it is. My appreciation goes to the whole team at Quill Tree Books for being such a wonderful home for *Meet Me at Blue Hour*.

Thank you to the Canada Council for the Arts for supporting me in writing this book.

One of the greatest joys of my author life is the community that surrounds me. To the booksellers, librarians, bookstagrammers, and fellow writers who have made my life richer by being in it—you consistently reaffirm my belief that book people are the best people.

To my friends—both in and out of publishing—I'm grateful for your presence and for the opportunity to be in your orbit. Special shout-out to Axie Oh, Sunni Chen, Corey Liu, and Genki Ferguson. Thank you for the laughs, the friendship, and for being creatives who always inspire me!

Graci Kim, Jessica Kim, Susan Lee, and Grace Shim— you are my people. Though this book has gone through many changes, I will never forget that its early brainstorms included you around a table with a box of mochi donuts and a view of the sea.

Thank you to Sarah Harrington, Grace Li, and Carly Whetter for being the best godmothers a book could ever have. You are some of my favorite people to talk story with.

To my family—아빠, 엄마, 언니, 오빠, John, 세연언니, Emory, Jonah, and Chloe. At the lowest points of writing this book, you were a balm to my soul just by being there, as you are. I love you!

And of course, to Sue O, my number one supporter. Through every high and low—both in writing and in life—the greatest gift is being able to live it all with you by my side.

Lastly, to you, reader. This book is no longer just mine, but ours, and I feel so grateful to share that with you. Thank you for reading. Thank you, thank you, and thank you again.